STICKY FINGERS

Roger Collinson

Ⓐ

Andersen Press · London

First published in 1996
by Andersen Press Limited
20 Vauxhall Bridge Road, London SW1V 2SA

© 1996 by Roger Collinson

This edition first published in 2000
Reprinted 2001

The right of Roger Collinson to be identified as the author
of this work has been asserted by him in accordance with
the Copyright, Designs and Patents Act, 1988.

British Library Cataloguing in Publication Data available
ISBN 0–86264–969–2

Phototypeset by Intype London Ltd
Printed and bound in Great Britain by
The Guernsey Press Company Ltd., Guernsey,
Channel Islands

Cover illustrations © 1996 by Tony Ross

Contents

1   A Chance Encounter   7

2   Jackpot   11

3   More Than Meets the Eye   18

4   An Uninvited Caller   29

5   The Unhappiness of Cousin Terry   38

6   Elspeth Forces the Pace   42

7   First Blood to Voules   48

8   Thinking Caps   54

9   Enter Auntie Efful   60

10   Quick Change Artist   70

11   A Clash of Cultures   76

12   A Dog's Dinner   81

13   A Painful Confession   88

14   Punch-Up!   95

15   Epilogue   108

1

A Chance Encounter

Life is like wandering blindfold through a minefield.
Well, that's how Buzz Beecham sees it following
those bizarre events which climaxed in the riot at
the Summer Fayre. Even before this trauma, Buzz
had always been a steady boy, preferring quiet and
routine while others thirsted for adventure. And so
it is not surprising that now he hopes for nothing
more exciting than a pension and a few insurance
policies.

To understand what has left him prematurely
middle-aged, we must retrace our steps through
time to a summer's afternoon a year ago, when he
was waiting at the bus-stop after school. The day
had brought with it nothing out of the ordinary, and
the evening promised only some French irregular
verbs to memorise and a history essay: 'Why I
would or would not have cut off King Charles the
First's head'. Buzz, who had not the heart to swat
a fly, had no problem with his answer; but he was
worrying about how to spin it out for the minimum
two pages. For some reason, the simple statement
'Because it's not a nice thing to do' would not have
satisfied Miss Runecast.

Buzz was not alone as he waited for his bus. Had he been, then he would have escaped the tangled net in which he was to find himself enmeshed. At that time of day, of course, Buzz never was alone, being just one of a horde of pupils which lay in wait for omnibuses. He was alone only in the sense that he was not accompanied by any friend or classmate. His immediate neighbours chanced to be a bunch of Year Sevens. (Buzz was then at the end of his eighth year, as you might deduce from the length of wrist which hung below the cuffs of his shabby uniform.) These Year Sevens were conspicuously boisterous, confirming Buzz in his opinion that the younger generation was going to the dogs. They jostled one another; they fell against Buzz without apology; they exchanged improper jokes which he pretended not to understand; they shouted coarse abuse at passers-by; and one of them – a burly boy – who had been munching an apple, hurled the core back down the queue, careless of where the juicy missile fell. Buzz wished that he could get away from them; but this would have meant giving up his place at the very front and going to the back; and that would almost certainly have meant his not getting on the first bus which came along. And so he stood his ground.

At last, a double-decker rolled into view and, with squealing brakes and a cloud of diesel fumes, it pulled up at the stop. Normally, the Corporation buses were operated driver-only, but, at this time of the day, a second employee rode shot-gun. And, when the hydraulic doors hissed open, it was to reveal the familiar and formidable person of Big Bertha. Life on the buses had soured the lady's nature; and, looking at her now, it was hard to believe that her interests had once been pressing flowers and country dancing.

The masses behind Buzz surged forward, and he found himself thrust against the unyielding barrier of Big Bertha, whose granite figure blocked the entrance. Her language was a model of economy. It would not have filled two lines – far less two pages.

'You *shove*, kid,' she said, 'and you're *orf*! . . . *See*?' As she spoke, she prodded Buzz with her forefinger for greater emphasis.

Excuse and explanation were not an option; so Buzz meekly nodded and, as Big Bertha pivoted her frame slightly to the left, he squeezed through the gap with the Year Sevens treading on his heels. Buzz scrambled up the stairs, eager to secure the best seat at the front. This he did; but his triumph was short-lived as the gang of Year Sevens flung themselves after him onto the same seat – designed to accommodate three sober adults, not five minors.

The bus filled and then lurched on its rowdy way. But the noise of Buzz's junior companions rose above the general hub-bub. Their laughter was more raucous; their shouts more deafening; their shrieks more piercing; and their feet hammered on the floor above the driver's head. It was more than fully evolved human flesh and blood could stand. The bus shuddered to an unscheduled halt, and Big Bertha laboured to the upper deck and stood over the occupants of the coveted front seat.

'*Orf*!' she said.

The leader of the Year Seven gang – whose nickname Buzz had learnt was Fingers – did half open his mouth to deliver a gem of witty repartee, but, catching the look in Big Bertha's eye, thought better of it. Followed by his mates and without a word, he clattered down the stairs. Sighing with relief, Buzz sank back into his seat.

'Orf! . . . I've warned *you* before . . . Now, orf!'

Buzz blinked and gaped up at Big Bertha, slow to grasp that it was he she was addressing.

'*Orf*!' she said once more; and the menace in her voice raised Buzz's hair.

'But . . . but . . .' he stammered, getting weakly to his feet. He was conscious of being the object of forty pairs of eyes, of forty breaths held in eager anticipation of some *action*. Cowed by the balance of power so unfairly weighed against him, he followed Fingers' example and left without an exit speech.

2

Jackpot

The Year Sevens were still standing on the pavement when Buzz stepped off the bus; and, as that vehicle pulled away, Fingers gestured savagely to the gawping passengers. Buzz wondered if this was how he had earned his nickname. An elderly lady stopped to remonstrate with him.

'And does your mother know that you behave like this?' she asked severely.

'Nah!' said Fingers.

'Well, young man, just remember God sees everything you do!'

'Yeah,' Fingers agreed with her. 'But 'e ain't gonna tell no one!'

Tutting and shaking her head in disbelief, the lady hurried on her way.

Before Buzz had time to gather his thoughts and decide what was best to do, the first fat drops of a summer shower splatted on his head. He had no coat, and at Marie Lloyd Comprehensive umbrellas were definitely not the thing. The Year Sevens were similarly without protection from the elements, and it was then that Fingers displayed his undoubted qualities of leadership.

''Ere, Goggles! You got any dosh?' he said to Buzz.

'Er, well, yes. I suppose I have,' Buzz answered, too taken aback to ask Fingers what business it was of his.

'Right! In the caff, ev'ryone!' Fingers ordered. And Buzz was swept into the café at whose doors the bus had dumped them. Before he could protest, he was seated at a table, and Fingers was calling on the proprietor for teas. A large, unsmiling man, he approached and put steaming mugs down on the plastic cloth.

''E'll pay,' said Fingers, jerking his head at Buzz.

If it occurred to Buzz to question this, he changed his mind when the café owner turned to him. Possibly related to Big Bertha, he rivalled her in bulk and charm; and so Buzz meekly counted the coins out from his purse.

'An' wot they call ya?' Fingers asked, when he had refreshed himself with noisy mouthfuls of the tea.

'Richard,' Buzz said.

'Richard Wot?'

'Richard Beecham.'

'An' wot d'yer mates call ya?'

'Buzz,' said Buzz.

'*Buzz*? . . . Oh, yeah, I gittit. Buzz *Bee*cham! . . . Good, innit? . . . Well then, me old fruit, Buzz it is. Right?'

Buzz didn't think there was anything at all right

about the familiar way this Year Seven kid spoke to him. But it was better than being addressed as 'Goggles'. And so he sipped his tea and pondered the best course of action when the rain had ceased. His bus pass was valid only if he boarded at the school stop, and the greater part of his spare cash had just gone on teas for Fingers and his chums. If he was not to be penniless for the rest of the week, he could look forward to a long walk home.

'That fruit-machine,' Fingers said, 'is just about ready to cough up.'

'Eh?' said Buzz, bringing his mind back to the present. 'What?'

'That there fruit-machine . . . be'ind ya.'

Buzz twisted round and saw, in a corner of the café, a fruit-machine winking its spendthrift invitation.

'I've got a feelin' for 'em,' Fingers boasted. 'An' I reckon a few more goes an' . . . *bingo*! 'Ere, lend us a couple of ten-ps, Buzz.'

'Well, I don't know . . .' Buzz began to say, too shy to refuse outright.

'Oh, come on!' Fingers said. 'Ya can't take it wiv ya!'

Not if you get your hands on it, thought Buzz. But, finding himself stared at for his miserliness, he took out his purse again and extracted two ten-p pieces, which he put into Fingers' out-stretched palm.

The Year Sevens left the table and besieged the fruit-machine. Buzz followed, anxious to keep track of his investment.

'Go it, Fingers!' the largest of Fingers' supporting cast piped up. He was a boy who in stature already far exceeded Buzz, and, having been baptised 'Timothy', was inevitably known as 'Tiny'.

'Yeah! Go it, Fingers!' the others cried.

Fingers inserted a coin, blew on his finger-tips, rubbed his hands together, and, with practised concentration, pulled the handle. Drums bearing the pictures of various fruits whirled round until, one by one, they fell still. But no line of lemons, oranges or cherries. Buzz heard the ten-p fall into that chamber reserved for squandered wealth, and the Year Sevens groaned. Then Fingers made himself ready for another go. Again the fruits revolved, and again Buzz heard his money drop beyond recovery, which was no more than he had feared all along. But Fingers was one of life's optimists.

'Gi's anuvver,' he demanded.

'But,' said Buzz, 'you've just lost two. I shan't have any left.'

'So wot ya gonna do?' Fingers reasoned. ''Ang on to a bit of loose change, or 'ave a go at gettin' yer 'ands on some dosh worth 'aving? . . . Ya gotta speculate to accumulate.'

Buzz was not convinced, but he surrendered the last ten-p he had.

'Cheer up, cock!' said Fingers. 'When I've cracked this, you'll need 'alf-a-dozen purses.'

Buzz envied him his confidence; but he could not help feeling a kind of satisfaction when, for the third time, Fingers failed to hit the jackpot.

'Right,' said Fingers quietly. 'This one's gonna need a little extra 'elp.'

'What d'you mean?' Buzz asked, wondering anxiously how much this was going to cost him.

'Oh, just a little trick me Cousin Terry taught me.'

'Is 'e the one who's doin' time?' asked another of Fingers' henchmen, a boy whose T-shirt, like the café tablecloths, seemed to be a record of all the eatables and drinkables that had passed over it that day.

'All right, Toe-Rag, all right!' Fingers hissed between clenched teeth. 'No need to broadcast it!'

This reference to 'doing time' sent Buzz's unease rocketing off the graph into the realms of total panic. He was consorting with criminals! . . . or with the younger cousins of criminals! He decided he had better put all those ten-ps down to experience, cut his losses, and get out. And so, while Fingers was occupied in muttering instructions to his accomplices, Buzz edged back to their table to retrieve his bag. He had it in his hand and was on the point of making his escape, when he heard Fingers give the order: '*Now*!' At his word, Tiny, Toe-Rag, and the weedy boy called Picker, who were

15

standing to one side of the machine, gave it a sharp and vigorous shove so that it tilted. At the same time, Fingers, with a snappy wrist action, pulled and pushed the handle. Cousin Terry would have been proud of his pupil – had he been at liberty to watch him – for the consequence of his little trick was a deluge of ten-p coins cascading from the machine. But the proprietor of the café was wise to the likes of Cousin Terry, and he had fitted an alarm which went off if his fruit-machine was interfered with. And now it filled the café with its din.

Buzz stood, dazed and paralysed by the pandemonium let loose. But Fingers was equal to the situation.

'Scarper!' he shouted, and headed for the door. He was followed by the others. And Buzz, seized by the primitive instinct for flight, found himself chasing after them. He was the last out of the café, and, without thinking, he took his lead from Fingers' gang. He splashed through puddles, dodged between pedestrians, and ducked round corners. At last, Fingers stopped in the doorway of a shop which was closed and boarded up. For some time the boys were speechless, gasping to regain their breath.

'Blimey!' panted Fingers. 'Who'd 'ave thought it? . . . Still, at least we've covered our expenses.' And he pulled a handful of silver from his pocket.

This was when Buzz got angry. Hadn't he been thrown off a bus; hustled into buying teas; bullied into parting with his cash for gambling; made a party to an attempt to cheat the café owner, and, finally, become a fugitive from justice? As with a lot of quiet and timid people, it took anger to give Buzz enough bottle to stand up for himself.

'Just what do you mean . . . "*our* expenses"?' he demanded. 'I'm the only mug who's spent a penny!'

'Okay! Okay, squire!' said Fingers. 'Don't get yer knickers in a twist! . . . *There's* yer tea-money, and *'ere's* the thirty-p ya put in the machine.' This still left a tidy sum which Fingers slipped back into his pocket. Buzz was not satisfied.

'And what about all *that*?' he asked.

'My commission,' Fingers explained. 'Professional services . . . you know.'

Buzz did not know. But he had calmed down enough to realise that, having got his money back, his best plan now was to leave Fingers before he could be caught up again in any of his dodgy schemes.

'*Hmmmph*!' he sniffed, and left the Year Sevens without another word. He found his way back to the bus route, bought a ticket, and arrived home late.

Irregular French verbs and the rights and wrongs of chopping off King Charles's head occupied the remaining hours. And when in bed Buzz mused on the day's misadventures, he comforted himself with the thought that Fingers and his cronies, together with the martyr king, were history.

17

3

More Than Meets the Eye

Buzz woke, next morning, revived and almost hopeful, with a day in prospect which threatened nothing worse than P.E. with Mad Max. Mind you, it would be hard to imagine anything that could be worse; and 'Rembrandt' Zilesnick, the form forger, made a steady income out of supplying sick-notes for the ones Mad Max had it in for. Buzz knew that he was on Mad Max's short list; and, if any member of the current victim-squad fell by the way, his name could well fill up the vacancy. Buzz was particularly concerned for Evelyn Sweet, a sensitive boy, who was not cut out for the kind of rough horse-play and graduated tortures which was Mad Max's concept of a P.E. lesson. It was hard enough his being called 'Sweetie' all the time by an Australian thug with the power of life and death; but to be challenged, week in and week out, to prove his manhood by doing a bungee-jump of fifty metres on a length of elasticated rope which would stretch to fifty-one was just too much. Buzz feared that one day Evelyn might attempt it. And then what would become of him – of *Buzz* that is?

He was occupied in gloomy thought and toying

with a bowl of cornflakes, when his mother spoke.

'You're going to be late . . . Elspeth left long ago.'

I have delayed introducing Elspeth into this little narrative. It seemed inhumane to spring her on the unsuspecting reader within the first few pages. Buzz, on the other hand, had had a lifetime to reconcile himself to her existence.

Elspeth was Buzz's sister, his senior by eighteen months. Now, in fairness, I admit that, in suggesting that Elspeth could be likened to a piece of grit in the eye or to a sharp stone in your shoe, I am voicing Buzz's opinion. But his was not the universal judgement. The world at large praised Elspeth for: her intelligence, her industry, her sense of responsibility, her etcetera, etcetera. And Buzz was bidden to model himself on Elspeth in everything except her taste in dresses. Not that I would have you think that Buzz was a great disappointment to his parents. But he suffered by comparison with that paragon of all the virtues, Elspeth. Loved and admired was Elspeth by Mum and Dad, grandparents, aunts, uncles, cousins, friends, and schoolteachers. But she got right up Buzz's nose.

Well, the good news was that Elspeth had already put some time and space between herself and Buzz. The bad news was that there was precious little time for Buzz to close the space between himself and Marie Lloyd. Abandoning the cornflakes, he snatched up his case and hurried to the bus-stop.

19

He arrived at school with just a minute or two in hand. Students thronged the gates and Buzz was just one more figure in a tide of yuck-green blazers which flowed sluggishly into the yard. Garish banner-posters, attached to the security railings, announced the Summer Fayre, and listed among its attractions a Display of Gymnastics, the Mile End Majorettes, and a Dog Show.

Buzz ignored all this publicity, but he did notice a police car parked at the steps to the main entrance. This was by no means unusual, and it was only later that he accessed the fact from the data-banks of memory. What did register with him and brought him up sharp was seeing Fingers, flanked by Picker, Toe-Rag and Tiny, clearly on the lookout for someone. Then, on catching sight of Buzz, Fingers bared his teeth in greeting.

'Wotcher, Buzz, me old mate!'

Alarm manifested itself in the churning of Buzz's stomach, in the icy sensation trickling down his spine, and in the colour draining from his cheeks. The Year Sevens surrounded him, and Fingers threw wide his arms.

''Ow ya doin', Buzz? . . . Tiny, take Buzz's case for 'im . . . Nice to see ya, Buzz!' As the case was wrenched from Buzz's hand, Fingers draped one of his extended arms around Buzz's shoulder and led him on. 'I bin finkin', old fruit – and don't say *there's a first time for ev'rything* – 'cos I know wot a wicked

20

sense of humour you 'as – an' I reckon I got me
sums wrong yesterday. I reckon you ought to 'ave
anuvver quid out of our winnin's.'

So saying, he pressed the cash on Buzz, who
struggled with the ethics of the case. Was he entitled
to this money? Was it profiting from the proceeds
of a crime? . . . But it is hard to refuse cash which
people push into your hand. (The literature of
Ancient Rome played little part in the curriculum
at Marie Lloyd; had it been otherwise, Buzz might
have recalled the bitter lesson the Trojans learned:
'to fear Greeks even when they bring gifts.') And
Buzz decided it was some compensation for all the
inconvenience he had suffered; and, instead of
asking himself what was in it for Fingers, he
pocketed the coins. Just then the bell rang.

'Right, Tiny,' said Fingers, looking back, 'you can
give Buzz 'is case now . . . Ta-ta, Buzz. 'Ave a nice
day!'

And Fingers and his minions were gone. Buzz
struggled through the corridors and up the stairs to
his form-room for registration, and then fought his
way back down again to the Hall for the assembly.

The compere at these daily gatherings was usually
one of the senior teachers. But, this morning, the
dais, with its illuminated lectern and its microphone,
was occupied by no less a person than the Head
herself. If Big Bertha was, in her own way, a woman
of forceful personality, no less so was Mrs Tyte-

21

Knightley, M.A., B.Ed., O.B.E. Mrs Tyte-Knightley was conspicuously capable. *Capable of anything*! her male subordinates muttered together in the men's washroom, with the taps turned full on and the hand-drier blowing. She was to staff-management, they felt, what King Herod was to playschools. And Mrs Tyte-Knightley's rule was not only absolute among her teachers. She reigned with a rod of iron over fifteen-hundred pupils, and her undercover intelligence was such that it was rumoured that each tutor-group contained a member of the thought-police.

And there she stood: hair groomed to wig-like perfection, crisply starched white blouse, black skirt, academic gown – and those unblinking eyes, which, no matter how big the group before her, always seemed to be staring straight at *you*. Buzz tried to avoid her gaze without looking shifty. Did she know already about the quid Fingers had just given him? He wished, now, he had refused it.

When the last-comer had shuffled to his seat, Mrs Tyte-Knightley spoke. The sound system was excellent, and the effect was very intimate; which was far more unsettling than if you felt you were just one of a crowd being harangued from a distant platform.

'I have observed before,' Mrs Tyte-Knightley crooned, 'that each of us is an ambassador for the School, wherever we are, whatever we do. Either we add lustre to the name of Marie Lloyd, or we besmirch it . . .' She paused to allow her audience to meditate on this. 'It pains me, therefore,' she continued, 'to report that, last night, because of their misconduct, a group of boys was ejected from the bus in which they travelled. And then, on the pavement, so far forgot themselves that a member of the public has complained to me . . . Perhaps the persons concerned will now identify themselves?'

Buzz gripped his seat, repeating in his mind, again and again: 'I didn't do anything! I didn't do anything!' He was too occupied in preventing himself from standing up with his hands in the air to wonder how Fingers and his sidekicks were responding to this appeal for frank confessions. The fact was that Picker was absorbed in playing with his bootlaces and did not hear what Mrs Tyte-Knightley was going on about; Toe-Rag – to be brutally honest – was unable to comprehend more than every third word she uttered; and Tiny's heart was very stony ground, unlikely to yield a rich harvest of repentance. But what of Fingers himself? What effect had Mrs Tyte-Knightley's eloquence on him? The answer is: none at all. For Fingers was elsewhere, at the time, being interviewed about matters of much greater moment.

'I am waiting . . .' Mrs Tyte-Knightley's voice purred like a leopardess in the anticipation of her lunch. Beads of perspiration stood out on foreheads and sweaty palms were rubbed down trouser legs. 'The whole school is waiting . . .'

It was too much for Nathan Slackwater, son of the local Baptist minister, a youth with a delicate conscience and highly suggestible. He sprang to his feet and, in a voice choking with remorse, cried out: 'It was me, Miss!'

In our courts of law, a confession must be supported by evidence before guilt can be established. But, at Marie Lloyd, Mrs Tyte-Knightley *was* the law; and, as long as a public sacrifice was offered to it, the niceties of justice could be set aside. And so, although it seemed improbable that this pale, skinny rabbit of a boy had danced on the public thoroughfare, mouthing oaths and making obscene gestures, he was dismissed from the Hall to await his doom. (The wrath of Pastor Slackwater and the heated interview he had with Mrs Tyte-Knightley do not concern us).

With the exit of Slackwater Junior, the tension among the rest of Marie Lloyd's sons and daughters eased; and, her lust for blood being satisfied, Mrs Tyte-Knightley turned her attention to the less emotionally charged topic of the Summer Fayre. It was, she said, not only important as a fund-raising event, but as a show-case for the school. And, just as she expected everyone of them to be present, so she expected everyone of them to remember their responsibilities as hosts on the occasion. She remarked that the new feature in that year's programme, the Dog Show, had already excited great interest in the district. Prayer was then offered for the spirit of industry, loyalty, and obedience; and the School was sent forth – perhaps to multiply, if the first lesson happened to be mathematics, but, most emphatically, under no other circumstances.

Buzz was not, as I have said, a boy who craved high drama and adventure; and, after the strains and stresses of the recent past, he was content to go with the flow of the day's timetable. Even the session with Mad Max proved pleasantly low-key as he was too taken up with fine-tuning his kamikaze performers for Saturday's event to bother with intimidating those who were poorly endowed with muscle tissue. The only thing which did give Buzz a twinge of worry was the rumour that the police had spent a long time talking to a Year Seven kid. Buzz recalled the car with the constabulary trimmings, and he could think of no more likely candidate in the seventh year for the privilege of helping with enquiries than Fingers. And what more likely subject for discussion than Cousin Terry's method for persuading fruit-machines to part with their accumulated savings? And would Fingers try to implicate him, Buzz, as an older accomplice? Buzz's anxieties in this respect were unfounded. Questions far weightier than the ungentlemanly tilting of a fruit-machine were on the agenda being investigated by Detective-Sergeant Sprockett (accompanied by W.P.C. Mavis Comfrey) and one

Jason Elvis 'Fingers' Valentine.

In mildly cheerful spirits Buzz Beecham joined the exodus when the final bell signalled a truce between teachers and the taught. And it came as something of a shock to find Fingers and his henchmen again waiting for him at the gates. *Something of a shock* – that is an understatement. In truth, it was then that Buzz felt that somehow he had stumbled into a waking nightmare. Were these evil figures to haunt him everywhere he turned? His powers of fancy roared into over-drive ... What did they want of him? ... Were they aliens? ... Were they agents of some satanic cult? ... Why, of all the pupils at Marie Lloyd, had he been singled out? Buzz's feet were rooted to the tarmac as Fingers advanced on him, smiling the same smile with which the crocodile had welcomed little fishes in.

'Well,' Fingers said, 'in a civilised society they'd limit the hours us kids 'as to work. But look at us! ... The teachers 'ave all knocked orf, but 'ave we? ... Not on yer nelly! Only hours an' hours of 'omework to look forward to.' Neither Fingers nor his companions, as it happened, was burdened with bags or books; but Fingers pursued his theme. 'I mean t'say, that there case of yours is just about pullin' yer arm out of its socket ... 'Ere, Tiny! Take old Buzz's case for 'im again ... We'll walk ya as far as the bus-stop, old fruit.'

26

'*No!* . . . No, thanks!' said Buzz; and he clutched his case in both arms. 'I can manage.'

But Tiny ignored his protest and took hold of the handle and tugged. Buzz resisted. And there they stood: Tiny tugging and Buzz clinging to his case. It was an unequal contest, which Buzz was bound to lose. But, just as Tiny was on the point of wrenching the case from his grasp, a voice about as soothing as the charge from an electric fence froze him in mid-tug.

'And just *what* do you think *you're* doing?'

Now, some people are born with it. Mrs Tyte-Knightley was one, and Big Bertha was one, and Elspeth – for it was Elspeth who had materialised at this dramatic moment – was another. And the *it* to which I refer is, of course, authority. Elspeth was born to take control; and it was odds-on that, in the fullness of time, she would become Commander-in-Chief of the S.A.S., or, at the very least, Governor of Holloway. Sorting out a handful of brawling schoolboys was, for her, no greater challenge than swatting flies.

Tiny gawped in disbelief. Toe-Rag's and Picker's expressions were the facial equivalents of question-marks. And Fingers, recognising a superior power, prepared to beat a tactical retreat. Buzz, himself, could not decide whether he would rather be the victim of juvenile delinquents or be rescued by the likes of Elspeth. But the choice was not his to

27

make. Elspeth spoke again.

'*You*' – she eyed Tiny as she might a joint of pork well past its sell-by date – 'let go of my brother's case . . . And *you*' – the contempt in her voice was that reserved by older sisters for their younger brothers – 'you come with me.'

Tiny, who was used to taking his instructions from Fingers only, glanced at him uncertainly.

'Leave it,' Fingers told him.

'But wot about the . . .?' Tiny began to ask.

'I said *leave it*! It don't matter.'

Tiny released his hold on Buzz's case, and he and the others followed their leader from the field of battle. Buzz, crimson with the shame of being escorted by his sister, walked half a step in Elspeth's wake.

'And what was all *that* about?' Elspeth asked over her shoulder.

'Dunno,' Buzz answered, honestly.

Elspeth said: 'You ought to be playing with children of your own age.'

And *you*, thought Buzz, ought to be pickled in a bottle of formaldehyde.

4

An Uninvited Caller

The perceptive reader will suspect already that Buzz's case has a more important role in this affair than that of mere, incidental detail. So let us examine Buzz's case to try to discover what value it could hold for the likes of Fingers and his associates.

As a case, Buzz's case was unremarkable, except in being of a type not common among the bag-toting classes at Marie Lloyd. The most popular model was the sports or air-line hold-all: soft in its contours and ideal for the stuffing-in of shorts, singlets, leotards, trainers, fast foods, and so on. Less suited for the accommodation of papers, books and files. Buzz, when the time had come for him to move from his primary school to the halls of secondary education, had been presented by his grandparents with a case which made no bones about its job in life being the carrying of books. It was constructed of stout black artificial leather, and it opened at the top like a doctor's bag. Inside, it was divided into three compartments, and there was a fourth compartment on the outside of the case which was fastened by a zip and designed to hold only a copy of the *Financial Times*. Buzz did not read the *Financial*

Times and he never used this fourth compartment. He had tried to enliven the forbidding, funeral-director appearance of the case with stickers: 'Save the Whales', 'Greenpeace', 'I've Been to Euro-Disney' (which he hadn't), 'You're Looking at Genius', and the like. Nothing in all this would account for the sudden interest in the case that Fingers' gang had shown. And, for a little longer, it must remain a mystery.

The bus journey in Elspeth's company was uneventful – Life thought twice when Elspeth was about – and Buzz arrived home in good time for tea. But no sooner had he gone inside the house than a shifty little figure, which had followed him all the way from school, slid from behind a pillar box and studied the number on his door.

'Thirteen,' muttered Fingers to himself. 'Well, that's unlucky for some!' And, with this prophetic utterance, he quit the scene. Now, if you are of a superstitious cast of mind, your anxiety for Buzz's welfare will be heightened when I inform you that the day was Friday and the date the Thirteenth of July.

As I have just said, it was Friday; and for Buzz this meant that school work could be put aside for the better part of eight-and-forty hours and Sloth Rule O.K. And so, as was his custom after Friday tea, Buzz sank into a chair before the television, happy in the anticipation of an evening of unselective viewing. Elspeth was already upstairs doing her hour's violin practice as a reminder that man must not look for perfect rest in this life. And, as Elspeth sawed and scraped away at her Grade Eight studies, Buzz watched 'The News'. Wars, droughts, and slanging-matches in the House of Commons were broadcast nationwide, followed by the regional reports.

In London, top-billing was given to an escape from prison. The mug-shot of a convict scowled out of the screen at Buzz. It was the photographic portrait of a young man you would not willingly offend. The lowness of his forehead was compensated by a generous quantity of jaw; and the eyes, if not intelligent exactly, suggested that their owner knew a thing or two. Terrence Kidd had been serving time for his part in a raid on a diamond merchant in Hatton Garden. Although he had been caught, not all the stolen jewels had been recovered. Kidd had got away from prison hidden in a refuse lorry, and it was thought that he would try to return to the area in north-east London where he was known to have family and contacts in the underworld. He had a record of violence, and the public were warned not to approach him. Then, after reports of a collapsed sewer and of a giant marrow grown by a pensioner on the balcony of his sixteenth-storey flat, there was a round-up of events organised for the weekend. And the Marie Lloyd

Summer Fayre got a mention.

As Buzz sat there, a certain something was troubling his peace of mind. And it wasn't the fall in the stock-market, and it wasn't the proposed increase in V.A.T. No, it was something to do with the picture of that convict ... What was his name? ... Kidd? ... Yes, Terrence Kidd ... That was it ... And then Red Alert flashed and hooted in Buzz's brain, and the adrenalin surged round his system. *'Cousin Terry ... who was doing time ... the police interviewing a Year Seven boy.'* And again Buzz could see Fingers with that smile as friendly as a chain saw: *'Wotcher, Buzz, me old mate!'* Fingers pressing money on him. Fingers insisting on Tiny carrying his case ... Oh, there was more to all this than a good deed for the day. Whatever else Fingers might or might not be, he was not a card-carrying member of the Be-Kind-to-Buzz-Beecham Society.

So lost was Buzz in feverish speculation about the affairs of Fingers and his Cousin Terry, that he did not notice the peace which had descended on the house when Elspeth had completed her workout on the fiddle. Buzz's parents, who had joined him in the lounge, looked up in welcome as their daughter entered.

'Finished your practice, dear?' asked Mrs Beecham.

If Buzz had posed the same question, Elspeth would have raised an exasperated eyebrow; but she

32

only smiled sweetly at her mother.

'Not long now to your exam,' added Mr Beecham.
Elspeth agreed. Just ten more days.

'And then there's the School Concert,' said Mrs
Beecham. 'I'm really looking forward to that. It's a
busy time, isn't it? And there's the Fayre tomorrow.
Have you got a special job this year?'

'Yes,' said Elspeth. 'Oh, Richard, that reminds
me . . .'

'Eh? What?' Buzz asked, jerked back from the
sinister fantasies which occupied his thoughts to
the concrete horror of his sister.

'I said: "Oh-Ri-chard-that-reminds-me",' Elspeth
repeated with careful diction. 'Julia Bainbriggs and
I volunteered to sell tickets outside Madame Za-
Za's kiosk; but now Julia's gone down with a nasty
attack of irritable bowel syndrome, so I told Mr
Voules not to trouble about finding someone else.
You would help me.'

Buzz opened his jaws as a preliminary to protest,
but words did not come up to the starting-tape in
time.

'Do stop gaping like that!' said Elspeth. 'People
really will believe there's something wrong with
you.'

'But . . .' The speech for the defence got no
further.

'You've no other commitments at the Fayre, so
you might just as well make yourself useful by giving

me a hand as wander about getting in the way.'

'Both of you . . . *together*!' cried Mrs Beecham. 'That's nice.' In the teeth of all the evidence to the contrary, she still believed warm bonds of affection united her two children.

'And we'll take your school case,' Elspeth continued. 'It will do very well to put the money in out of sight. You can't be too careful on these occasions.'

'Now, you look here!' said Buzz. So Elspeth looked, unblinking, in his direction. 'I mean . . . well . . . you've no right . . . and . . . well . . . blow it! . . . I won't!'

Elspeth did not reply at once. She waited as though not certain that Buzz had made his point. Then, in a voice totally devoid of passion, she enquired: 'Do I take it, then, that you will tell Mr Voules tomorrow that you are backing out?'

'*Backing out*!' Buzz exclaimed.

'Well, that is how it will seem to Mr Voules,' said Elspeth. This was a knock-out blow. Elspeth knew it. Buzz knew that she knew it. She knew that Buzz knew that she knew it.

Mr Voules was Mrs Tyte-Knightley's first lieutenant. And, while his mistress maintained an aloofness, a regal mystique, Voules fulfilled her will; not with jack-boot and rhino-whip literally, but he was not a man to be lightly thwarted. It would not be beyond Voules, for example, to put it into the head of Mad Max that one Buzz Beecham would benefit

34

from a personalised programme of physical education. Elspeth took Buzz's silence to mean that she had won him round to her way of seeing things.

Mrs Beecham, who was ignorant of the dangerous currents which ran beneath the surface of this brief exchange, asked: 'Who's Madame Za-Za?'

'She's a fortune-teller,' Elspeth said. 'A professional. The School is going to get half of what she takes.'

'A load of codswallop!' declared Mr Beecham. ' "Tall dark strangers . . . a change in your circumstances" . . . and anything else that'll give the punters a thrill! You wouldn't think in this day and age people would pay good money for a lot of old baloney!'

'Oh, I don't know, Leonard,' said Mrs Beecham. 'Mrs Wainwright – her at Number Twenty-Two – went to this clairvoyant when her cat was missing. And she told her that "what was lost would be restored with interest". And do you know what? . . . A week later that cat turned up at the backdoor with *four kittens*!'

'That don't prove nothing,' said Mr Beecham. 'And you won't catch *me* crossing this Madame Hoo-Ha's palm with silver!'

'Bronze or notes,' Elspeth corrected him. 'A consultation with Madame Za-Za costs five pounds.'

'*Five* . . .!' Mr Beecham was speechless. 'And some of us actually work for a living!'

For some time the argument went round in circles . . . and it would have been interesting to know if Madame Za-Za could have predicted the disturbed night the Beecham household suffered.

Buzz slept at the front of the house and, during the hot and airless nights of summer, he kept his window open. It was about two in the morning that he was woken by noises. With Buzz it was as it is with most people when they are dragged from the depths of slumber. He knew that he could hear something but he could not, at first, identify it. Then he realised it was a mixture of noises. There was heavy breathing, for one thing; the scraping of boots against brickwork for another; and muttered oaths for a third. Buzz was, by now, tinglingly awake from his toe-nails to the pimple on his nose; and he stared in a paralysis of fear at the open window through which moonlight shone atmospherically. The sounds of strenuous effort grew louder, and then the fingers of a right hand reached up for Buzz's window-sill.

At that moment, came a cry of alarm; the fingers vanished; and, from below, came the clanking of metal striking stone; the clatter of an over-turned dustbin; the smashing of milk bottles; and more uninhibited blasphemy. Finally, there was the noise of feet running off down the street.

By this time, the whole family was awake, and,

when Mr Beecham ventured outside to investigate, he found the drainpipe which passed close to Buzz's window lying in three pieces and further damage consistent with the falling of a heavy body. He deduced, as did the police when they arrived, that someone had attempted to enter the house – with criminal intent, it was assumed.

'Well, if there's anything worth pinching here,' said Mr Beecham, 'I wish they'd show me where it is.'

Buzz was questioned about what he had seen and heard; but his glimpse of the fingers of one hand was not going to help a police artist to build up an identikit picture of the would-be burglar. Buzz had his suspicions, even though he could think of no earthly reason why Cousin Terry should try to effect an entrance into the house. But he could not mention Fingers and his family to the police without the risk of fruit-machines finding their way into the investigation. And he kept his suspicions to himself.

5

The Unhappiness of Cousin Terry

North north-east of 13 Sebastapol Terrace, at a distance of two-and-a-quarter miles, lay a den of iniquity, a thieves' kitchenette that boasted none of that good order and sparkling cleanliness which characterised Mrs Beecham's house. Here, at a plastic-topped table, stained with the record of innumerable mugs of tea, were seated a man and a boy. A boy, that is, in years and stature, but in all else the equal of his companion. The reader will have no difficulty in identifying this juvenile as Fingers. His partner might be recognised from the photograph shown on television the previous evening; but, compared with the live original, that photograph was more like a publicity portrait for a dating agency. In fairness to Cousin Terry, it must be allowed that no man's disposition and appearance are much improved by his fall from a down-pipe being broken by a dustbin and a privet hedge. Cousin Terry was, he confided to his young relative, black and blue all over. And his vocabulary, limited at the best of times, was monotonously concentrated by recollection of the experience.

Now, I do not belong to that school of writing

which insists that, in the interest of Truth, every word spoken by one's characters must be spelt out. But, to convey something of the temper and the rhythm of Cousin Terry's discourse, I will substitute the inoffensive *something* where Cousin Terry repetitively employed an uncouth epithet of Anglo-Saxon ancestry.

'I'll tell ya, Fingers, straight up,' said Cousin Terry, for the umpteenth time, 'I *something* thought I'd *something* 'ad it!'

Fingers sucked his teeth in noisy sympathy.

'When that *something* drainpipe came *something* down, I could've *something* sworn it was *something* Endsville for your Terry-boy.'

'Nasty!' said Fingers.

'Yeah! *Something* was! And I'm *something* black an' blue all *something* over!'

'So ya said,' Fingers admitted.

'An' we still ain't got the *something* stone back! Wot the *something something* made ya put it in that kid's *something* case?'

'I've explained already,' said Fingers, wearily. '*You* give it to *me* to look after in case the Old Bill caught ya wiv it. Then, when I see their motor outside School, I guessed they'd come to put the squeeze on me. So I 'id it where no one'd never fink of lookin' ... An' I'd 'ave got it back at 'ome time – except this kid's big sister went an' stuck 'er 'ooter in.'

'Women!' snorted Cousin Terry. The best endeavours of feminists from Mrs Pankhurst to Germaine Greer had failed to change his mind-set. '*Women*!' he repeated, in case Fingers had not followed the complexity of his argument. Cousin Terry mused morosely on the mischief wrought in a man's world by women. 'Interferin' little . . .!'

'Yeah, yeah!' Fingers interrupted, not wishing to pursue the subject further. 'An' I did tell ya I didn't fink it wos a good idea to go breakin' into the 'ouse. The stone's safe enough where it is, an' I'll easy get me 'ands on it when the kid brings 'is case to School on Monday. I mean t' say, Terry, he's so green, *grass* couldn't teach 'im nuffin'!'

'I still don't *something* like it,' Cousin Terry grumbled. 'S'pose someone goes an' *something* nicks it?'

'Ain't no one gonna nick it!' Fingers said. 'Ain't no one knows it's there to be nicked! . . . 'cept Toe-Rag 'n Picker 'n Tiny, o' course. An' they ain't gonna tell . . . Look, I'll go an' keep an eye on the 'ouse the whole weekend. On Monday I'll get the stone back . . . an' then it's "'Bye, 'bye, Terry sweetheart! Send us a postcard from yer villa in South America!"'

Fingers had spoken shrewdly. Allusion to the El Dorado of Cousin Terry's dreams brought a loose smile to his troubled countenance, and the pupils of his eyes dilated at the vision of himself clad in monogrammed gold satin swimming-trunks, lounging by the Cousin Terry pool, glass in one hand, mega cigar in the other; and women in attendance – women fulfilling their proper function as his adoring handmaids. Yes, life would be *something* sweet when he'd sold the stone and had so much dosh that there weren't nothing what he couldn't buy . . . Then Cousin Terry's pupils contracted again. But 'e 'adn't got the stone! It was still in that kid's *something* case! . . . He glared at Fingers.

'All right!' said Fingers. 'All right! Keep yer 'air on! Ya know the plan. Ev'ryfing's under control . . . Now, while I'm away, you stay 'ere wiv Our Norman. The Old Bill don't know about Our Norman. An' don't go showin' yer face . . . Stay 'ere till I get in touch . . . Right?'

Cousin Terry's eyes rolled suspiciously at Fingers; but he had no alternative. 'Right,' he growled. 'But don't you go tryin' nuffin' clever . . . See?'

6

Elspeth Forces the Pace

This conference had taken place in the dawn light of Saturday. Though the sun had risen, the majority of law-abiding citizens had not. The Beechams, following the alarms and disturbances of the night, were still abed. It had taken Buzz some time to drop off again. That hand reaching up for his open window remained vivid in his memory. It was, he recalled, a large and hairy hand, not a hand to be trifled with. And, although police officers assured him there was no likelihood of the would-be burglar making a second attempt that night, he had closed and secured his window.

Sleep, when it did return to Buzz, was not the sort the poet has described as 'knitting up the ravell'd sleave of care'. On the contrary, grotesque figures pursued him through his fitful slumbers and did nothing to restore the jaded tissues. He woke, at last, sprawled on his back, the sheets twisted into ropes from which he fought to free himself. But, weary as he was, it was a relief to be back in the real world where even nasties like Elspeth were contained in time and space.

Feeling in want of reviving draughts of air, Buzz

stumbled across the room and drew the curtains, preparatory to flinging wide the casement. He gazed down into the street in that unfocused way with which one studies an all too familiar scene. But, in the same instant, he gasped and drew back as though he had been stung. It could not be! He was still dreaming! The strains and stresses he had suffered were making him hallucinate! Fingers would not – *could not* – be leaning against the lamp-post opposite the house at seven in the morning . . . Look again! Buzz sternly told himself. He peered round the curtain and sighed deeply with relief. The lamp-post stood there still where it had stood long before Buzz had walked this planet. And it stood alone, not supporting Fingers nor any other living soul.

Determined now to keep a firm grip on himself, Buzz decided on a shower – a cold one, perhaps. It would do wonders for his morale. He proceeded to the bathroom and arrived just in time to see Elspeth forestall him and to hear her bolt the door. So, with a good half-an-hour to kill, Buzz went down to the kitchen for a brew and the solace of digestive biscuits.

Buzz was one of Nature's dunkers, and his mug of tea soon had a deep sediment of sodden biscuit which had broken off before he could raise it to his lips. In the background, the local radio station did its best to distract listeners from anything which might be described as thought; for which Buzz was grateful, since his thoughts were still of a gloomy and an apprehensive turn. What with the disquieting images of Fingers and his Cousin Terry, and only the prospect of an afternoon's 'helping' Elspeth, life, Buzz felt, was anything but a bed of roses.

Over the radio, a cunningly edited tape produced a dog barking to the tune of 'Happy Birthday to You'. When the canine soloist had finished, a human voice, eager to share the secret of happiness, addressed the listening public. 'Yes! Make every day a birthday for *your* best friend, with Rover's Relish! Gourmet meals for the discerning dog . . . They're good-enough-to-eat!' A burst of enthusiastic yapping followed, and then the presenter of the programme continued: 'And the makers of Rover's Relish are sponsoring the Dog Show which is part of the Summer Fayre being held this afternoon in the grounds of the Marie Lloyd Comprehensive School. Winners in all classes – which includes a class for dogs with no class at all! – will receive, in addition to the trophies and cash prizes, a year's supply of Rover's Relish. So . . . o . . . o *be there*! . . . And the latest news about escaped convict, local bad lad, Terrence Kidd, is – that there is no news. The police have a theory that he's in hiding. And, since they can't find him, that sort of makes sense . . . And now, that way-out group, "The Camel's Hump", with their latest single, "Pardon

Me!" . . . Why, what have you done, lads?'

Mention of Cousin Terry had arrested Buzz at the critical moment of opening his jaws to receive a mouthful of dunked digestive, and the few seconds' delay as he listened to the bulletin was long enough for another deposit to plop into his mug. Cousin Terry might be in hiding, but he was near enough to come out at night like some East End Dracula and shin up Buzz's down-pipe. And then, in his mind's eye, Buzz saw again that dwarfish figure leaning against the lamp-post, and he knew that he had not been dreaming. But what interest could he, Buzz Beecham, hold for Fingers and his extended family?

The immediate effect of this anxiety was to make Buzz reluctant to leave the house. And so, although the sun had got his hat on and the birds and bees were hip-hip-hip-hooraying like billy-o, Buzz did not enter into the spirit of the popular song by going out to play. Instead, like a hunted beast, he skulked in the dim recesses of his lair and got under Mrs Beecham's feet. From time to time, he peeped furtively into the street, but he saw no one lurking there. This did not reassure him – and rightly so! For Fingers, who had not stopped blaming himself for his clumsiness in being spotted earlier, was now professionally concealed where he could observe unseen.

Time and tide, however, wait for no man; and

neither, that day, did the Marie Lloyd Summer Fayre. The hour must come when Buzz would have to venture forth in the cause of collecting the five-quids from Madame Za-Za's clients. He half-wished he himself could have had a consultation with the lady, then and there. But, mercifully perhaps, the future was hidden from him.

Elspeth, on the other hand, happily ignorant of the dark forces gathering, faced the day with her wonted confidence and brio. That is to say, she rode rough-shod over any plans Buzz might have made and brushed aside his objections with the indifference of a charging hippopotamus.

'Now the Fayre,' she reminded him, on the assumption that he was halfwitted, 'opens at *two*, when that woman who looks like the Queen arrives with her royal corgies. *You* should be there at Madame Za-Za's kiosk a quarter-of-an-hour before that – that's at *a quarter-to-two* – no later! I need to be at School by eleven to help in setting out the refreshment tent. Mr Voules has selected half-a-dozen of the more responsible pupils to lend a hand with that ... Oh, and I'll take your case with me, so that I *know* it will be there. Empty it now. I must leave in just ten minutes.'

Buzz meekly bent to the stiff breeze of her instructions. His case, without its load of academic junk, felt strangely light as he carried it to Elspeth's room.

'Leave it there,' said Elspeth, who was giving her blonde hair a final brushing before putting on the headband which would keep it tidy through all the exertions of the day. There was nothing for Buzz to wait for, and he wandered down to the kitchen in search of nibbles. A few minutes later, Elspeth's voice rang through the house in crisp farewell to her parents, and the slamming of the front door sealed her departure.

In the litter-basket in her room lay the stickers from Buzz's case. You could not expect Elspeth to walk along the open streets parading badges of adolescent protest and enthusiasms. But it forced Fingers into some immediate and quick thinking. From his point of vantage, he saw the kid's big sister come out of the house and set off up the street, swinging a black case, light-heartedly. Now, it was not black cases in general, but just Buzz's black case in particular which was of interest to Fingers. The case the big sister was swinging was the right sort of case, no doubt about that; but it was a case without stickers. Could it be the big sister's case? But Fingers remembered clearly that the day before she had been carrying a case of quite a different kind. Perhaps, then, it was the right case, but stripped of stickers. Elspeth was marching briskly on, and Fingers did not have time to consider further. He came to a decision, and set off in discreet pursuit.

47

7

First Blood to Voules

Fingers shadowed Elspeth to the bus-stop, where she waited, one foot tapping the pavement in her impatience, until a Number 641 arrived. He stood in the doorway of a butcher's shop while she boarded, and then leapt on just before the doors had closed. The bus was almost full, and the only empty seat was behind the one where Elspeth sat. Fingers was nervous – this much he admitted to himself – but he reasoned that Elspeth probably would not notice him, and that, if she did, she would most likely think nothing of it. His reading of her character was spot on: to the likes of Elspeth he was less than the dust beneath her chariot wheels. And, besides, she was far too wrapped up in her agenda for the day to give a second thought to the runty little boy who had brushed past her and now occupied the seat behind. Buzz's empty case rested on her knees, and Fingers' eyes rested on the case. It was Buzz's case, he was certain now, and he had to fight back a reckless impulse to seize it and make off with it. A foolish plan about which even Cousin Terry might have second thoughts.

When the bus halted at the stop which served

Marie Lloyd, Elspeth alighted; and, at a safe distance, Fingers followed her through the school gates and onto the playing fields where figures hurried to and fro, busy with preparations for the afternoon's event. Elspeth's steps led to a large marquee where tables and chairs had been set out for the convenience of weary visitors who sought refreshment.

Elspeth was greeted enthusiastically by several girls and by a tall man, dressed down for the occasion in pressed jeans and a Marie Lloyd T-shirt. His head was remarkable in appearing rather short of skin, so that what he had was stretched tightly over the bone, of which he had plenty. Any of Marie Lloyd's pupils could have told you that this was Mr Voules.

'Ah, Elspeth!' he said, with a toothy smile reserved for favourites. '*There* you are! . . . Now, girls, you'll find a pile of tablecloths beside the tea-urn on a trestle at the far end of the marquee. Our first task is to cover the tables with them. So let's get on with it! . . . Chop-chop!' His years as a cub in Beaver Patrol had left their mark.

Fingers, peering round the entrance to the marquee, watched Elspeth and her companions trip in an explosion of excited twittering to the store of table linen Mr Voules had indicated. He watched Elspeth put the case down on the ground beneath the trestle, take several cloths and begin to fling them expertly over naked tables. And the case stood there, unattended and unregarded. This, surely was a window of opportunity. But it was unthinkable for Fingers to tread openly down the length of the marquee. Not only would he be noticed, but he was known to Mr Voules. And, in Mr Voules's eyes, he – Fingers – was guilty. Guilty of *what* at any particular moment might be in question, but his chronic state of guilt was not. And, when it came to doing justice to 'Fingers' Valentine, Mr Voules was an ardent disciple of the Queen of Hearts: '*First* the sentence, and *then* the evidence.'

No, thought Fingers, a more oblique approach was called for. He withdrew his face and sauntered round the outside of the marquee to the further end. Then, glancing left and right to make sure he had not excited curiosity, he dropped to his knees and cautiously lifted the canvas. And there was the case, right in front of him, just half-a-dozen steps away. It would be easy to wriggle through and wriggle back, pulling the case after him. Then all he had to do was to extract the stone and scarper. A piece of cake!

Fingers watched maidenly pairs of legs in jeans and ski-pants negotiate the tables; and, what with the squeals, the giggles, and the flapping of table-cloths, there seemed little risk of his being seen. The iron was hot. Now was the time to strike. Using his elbows as he had observed commandoes do in

50

war films, he began to inch his way beneath the canvas wall and into the confines of the great marquee. The gap between him and the case narrowed by the second. A few wriggles more and he would grasp the prize. But so intently was Fingers' gaze fixed on the prize that he failed to keep a weather-eye on the movements of the enemy.

Not for nothing had Mr Voules risen in his profession to the dizzy heights of Mrs Tyte-Knightley's hit-man. His ability to inspire his pupils with a love of learning might be minimal, but he had the vigilance of a hawk with a ruthless appetite for lesser rodents. And he had been quick to notice Fingers' unorthodox and furtive entry. Skilled in the arts of guerilla warfare, Mr Voules slid stealthily round the perimeter of the tent, and he was standing right behind the prostrate Fingers when he spoke.

'Ah, Valentine!'

Fingers sprang up, struck his head upon the underside of the trestle table, and fell back to the ground.

'I fear,' continued Mr Voules, 'you are a little early for the beverages and home-made cakes with which our visitors are to be regaled this afternoon. But *then* there will be no need for you to "go upon thy belly" to obtain a cup of tea and a buttered scone . . . if the quest for such is what brings you here. Which I doubt!'

Mr Voules had dropped the tone of playful

banter, and his voice was dark with menace. Fingers gulped. Not because he feared physical assault. He knew the law and understood that, while he might attack Mr Voules with impunity, it was more than Mr Voules's job was worth for him to land him a fourpenny one. Nevertheless, it was all very inconvenient. Not only had he been thwarted when the case was within inches of his reach, but this could put the big sister on the alert; and, even more serious, old Voules might . . . Which was exactly what old Voules went on to do.

'Stand up, Valentine,' he said. Fingers stood, and Mr Voules lowered his head so that he was looking directly into Fingers' eyes, with only the length of a ball-point pen between them. '*Why* you are here I do not know. But I do know that, whatever the reason, it is bad news for Marie Lloyd. So take your evil little face away, and do not let me see it again before Monday morning, when I am paid – inadequately – to suffer it between the hours of nine and three-forty-five . . . You may leave by the conventional exit.'

This was a sound move on Mr Voules's part as Fingers had to pass beneath the scrutiny of Elspeth and the other girls, who regarded him with the distaste of diners finding a slug in the green salad. The inspection was long enough for Elspeth to recall that this was one of the boys that Buzz had been having trouble with the previous evening. But, when

52

Fingers was gone, she forgot about him and threw herself into the unpacking and setting out of cups and saucers, tea-spoons and plates.

Back at Number 13 Sebastapol Terrace, Buzz was calculating gloomily that it would soon be time for him to set off to School and to an afternoon of being bossed about by Elspeth in the service of horoscopy.

Back at Our Norman's, Fingers tried to persuade Cousin Terry yet again to keep his hair on. But Cousin Terry seemed hell-bent on baldness.

'*Something* teachers!' he complained. 'Why don't they mind their *something* business?' A question better men than he have often asked. Then Cousin Terry turned to Fingers. '*You* said the *something* stone was safe. And now it's *something* somewhere in a tent! I don't *something* like it, Fingers. And when I don't *something* like somefing, I get *something mad! ... Now, *you* get back to that *something* Fayre, and don't come *something* back wivout the stone, or somefing nasty will *something* 'appen to ya!'

'Right, Terry! Right!' said Fingers, edging to the door. 'I'm on me way.'

8

Thinking Caps

Fingers had never been a stickler for the truth; and his parting words to Cousin Terry were something less than honest. To return directly to the Fayre, as he had said he was going to, was out of the question. Some stratagem had first to be devised, and so he hurried to where Toe-Rag, Tiny and Picker would be found. They sat at a table in a burger-bar with a single portion of French-fries, passing the packet in strict rotation, and discussed Fingers' dilemma.

'Some'ow,' said Fingers, 'I've just gotta get back to School an' get 'old of that stone. Terry's turnin' nasty.'

'Does 'e thump?' asked Tiny, who looked up to Fingers' Cousin Terry as a role model.

'Yeah, that ... and other things,' Fingers answered, but he did not satisfy Tiny's curiosity in any detail.

Toe-Rag, who had been sitting wordless with his mouth hanging open, except when a chip was poked inside it, broke his silence.

'I don't see,' he said, 'wot the fuss is all about. It didn't look like a diamond to me. I mean, it weren't sparkly nor nuffin'.'

'That's 'cos it's an uncut diamond, dumbo!' Fingers told him wearily. 'It's not bin cut an' polished yet. But it's worth a fortune.'

'Oh . . . I see,' said Toe-Rag. But he didn't.

'Why can't ya just go in an' nick it?' Picker asked.

''Cos old Voules's eyes will be ev'rywhere. An', besides, that girl's 'ad a good look at me now. She'll scream blue murder if I go anywhere near 'er case.'

French-fries and the problem were digested. It was Picker who came up with the seminal idea.

'Can't ya disguise yerself?'

''Ow?' asked Fingers, irritably.

'Well . . .' said Picker, 'well . . . you could put a beard on.'

Fingers did not waste breath in answering.

'I see this film on telly last night,' said Toe-Rag.

'Oh, yeah,' said Fingers.

'It was an old one,' Toe-Rag went on. 'It weren't in colour.'

Toe-Rag's friends were used to his wandering off down the dead-end alleys of his own thoughts, and they took no notice.

'These two men was bein' chased by a gang, so they dressed up as women an' nobody knew, an' so they wasn't killed.'

'That's nice,' said Fingers.

Toe-Rag fell silent for a minute, and then he said, 'You could do that.'

'Do wot?' Fingers asked.

'Wot them men done ... Dress up as women ... well, as a girl. Then nobody wouldn't know ya.'

'Shall I thump 'im?' Tiny asked, eager for the practice.

'No ... not yet,' said Fingers, who, on second thoughts, was rapidly weighing the merits of Toe-Rag's suggestion. The prospect of going to the Fayre in drag was appalling. But what was the alternative? To return to Cousin Terry empty-handed? 'Wot could I wear?' he asked.

Picker and Tiny gasped as they realised that their leader was prepared to lay aside the dignity and glory of his manhood and to take upon himself the likeness of the weaker sex. The enormity of the disgrace was balanced only by the heroic dimensions of the sacrifice.

'Well?' Fingers repeated. 'Wot could I wear? ... You've got a sister ain't ya, Picker?'

'Eh? ... Oh, yeah!' Picker groaned, still struggling to come to terms with what had been proposed.

'Well, you get me some stuff, an' we'll meet in Tiny's shed.'

'Wot about yer 'ead, Fingers?' Picker asked.

'Me 'ead?' said Fingers. 'Wot about me 'ead?' His hand reached to his scalp and stroked the Number One which had left him virtually hairless. 'Well, bring me an 'at or somefing ... An' be quick about it!'

The shed in the backyard of Tiny's house was the gang's regular rendezvous. Here they smoked illicit cigarettes and pursued subjects and life-skills not included in the curriculum at Marie Lloyd. And here it was they were assembled when, thirty minutes later, Picker entered carrying a Sainsbury's plastic bag.

'It's the best I could do,' he panted, for he had been running. 'There ain't never no privacy in our place, and I only 'ad a minute to grab wot I could.'

'Well, wot ya got?' demanded Fingers.

From his bag, Picker pulled a white garment with a red cross on the front. 'An' there's an 'at wot goes wiv it,' he explained.

'It's a kid's nurse's dressin'-up kit!' Tiny protested.

'It wos the first thing 'anging in 'er cupboard,' Picker said. 'I told ya me mum was comin' up the stairs ... Oh, an' there's this as well. Thought it might come in useful.' From the bag he took a wig of blonde, curly hair. 'Our Tracy 'ad this skin disease last year an' all 'er 'air come out, so she wore this while it was growin' back again.'

Fingers had, thus far, kept silent; but now he burst out: 'A nurse's outfit! Wot are people gonna fink when they see me in a kid's nurse's outfit?'

'That's all right,' said Picker. 'I've bin finkin'. There's this fancy-dress competition. There'll be loads of kids dressed up. So, even if ya do look a bit funny, people'll just fink it's anuvver fancy-dress.'

'Ya could be right at that,' Fingers agreed. He glanced at his watch. 'Well, better get crackin'.'

A few minutes later and the world could see what it had been denied when, in the lottery of conception, a Y-chromosome had landed Mr and Mrs Valentine with a man-child rather than a maid. Fingers' sallow features were framed by Shirley Temple ringlets, and on top of the ringlets, at a saucy angle, perched a nurse's cap. His spindly legs, stripped of their encasing jeans, projected like sticks of celery from beneath the nurse's tunic, which on Fingers was of a daring mini-length. Toe-Rag and Tiny gazed in wonder at the transformation. But Picker could not suppress a snigger.

'It 'im!' said Fingers.

Tiny obeyed, instantly and expertly; and Picker doubled up, clutching his stomach.

'Sorry, Fingers,' he gasped. 'I didn't mean it ... Honest!'

'Serves ya right!' said Toe-Rag, nodding his head. 'It ain't nothin' to laugh at ... Any'ow, Fingers,' he went on, warming to his subject, 'I fink you're a bit of all right.'

'Shall I?' asked Tiny, hopefully.

'Nah!' said Fingers, who accepted Toe-Rag's diminished responsibility. 'But jus' you cut that out, Toe-Rag,' he warned.

Tiny now looked at Fingers' get-up critically.

58

'I ain't sure about the Doc Martens,' he confessed. 'Well, I ain't walkin' about barefoot!' Fingers snapped. 'Any'ow, all the birds are wearin' boots these days.' He took a deep breath, squared his rounded shoulders, and said, 'Right then! Let's go!'

9

Enter Auntie Efful

At the same time as Fingers, flanked by his companions, emerged onto the public thoroughfare, Buzz was standing at his front gate and peering nervously up and down the street. But Fingers – as we could have told him – was nowhere to be seen, and there was nothing on the horizon more alarming than an old lady trundling her wheelie-basket to the corner shop. Then Buzz, too, braced himself and set off to encounter Destiny on the playing fields of Marie Lloyd.

The day was perfect for a Summer Fayre. The sun shone in a cloudless sky, and gentle breezes blew, making the bunting flutter gaily and cooling visitors who might otherwise have become overheated and less willing to be parted from their money. And in their hundreds and in their thousands the crowds came flocking, eager to consume ice-cream, buy knick-knacks and white-elephants, gamble on Tombola and applaud such displays as were devised for their amusement. Over the public-address system, a tape of 'A Walk in the Black Forest' played its merry tune, and no one within a radius of half-a-mile could remain unaware that there was a happening at the School.

Elspeth, you will recall, had stipulated that Buzz should report for duty at one-forty-five; but, although he managed to arrive punctually almost to the second, it was to find that the public had anticipated the official opening at two and were already milling round the stalls and sideshows.

Madame Za-Za had her own booth of striped canvas, its entrance screened mysteriously by a beaded curtain. A board outside announced:

> **The World Famous**
> **MADAME ZA-ZA**
> **Reveals the Secrets of Your Future!**
> **Unrivalled in the casting of Horoscopes,**
> **Palmistry, Tarot Cards & Crystal Ball.**
> **'Consulted by the Stars about their Stars!'**

Elspeth was seated at a little table, with a book of tickets and a plastic margarine tub which held the float. Beneath the table was Buzz's case.

'I'm not late, am I?' Buzz asked.

'No,' said Elspeth. 'But it wouldn't have mattered if you were, since Madame Za-Za's not here yet.' You couldn't win with Elspeth. If Madame Za-Za had been there, he'd have been criticised for not having the initiative to come earlier. 'Oh!' And Elspeth brightened as she spoke. 'I think this must be her.'

'Ample' is the word to describe Madame Za-Za's figure, for Nature had given her second helpings of everything. But she carried herself with great dignity, looking neither to right nor left as she strode through the fun-seekers who wandered across her path. And it was as well she was a large and robust woman, for a lesser frame would have sunk beneath the weight of gold she carried on her person. Across her forehead was a heavy string of golden coins. Gold pendants, the size of lavatory pulls, swung from her ear-lobes. Gold chains hung in profusion round her neck. Gold rings, which could serve as knuckle-dusters, filled every finger. And her smile was like the opening of Fort Knox.

"Ullo, dearies!' she greeted Buzz and Elspeth. 'You must be my little 'elpers for the afternoon.' Her voice was husky, and her breath smelt like Buzz's neighbour, Mrs Wappit, who, Mrs Beecham claimed, was never off the gin. 'Just bin 'aving a spot of lunch,' said Madame Za-Za. 'You can't look into the future on an empty stomach. It's a terrible strain on the constitution. You've no idea!' She burped. 'Whoops! Pardon me! Must 'ave bin the pickles.' She steadied herself on Elspeth's table. 'Right, lovey, so you sell 'em a ticket, and when you see the last client come out you can tell the next one to come in ... Should do good business this afternoon, but you can't never tell.'

'Can't you?' Buzz asked. 'I'd have thought

you could.'

'Eh?' said Madame Za-Za. Then she erupted in a throaty laugh. 'Oh! I see what you mean!' She patted him playfully on the cheek. 'You're a proper caution, you are!' And, still chuckling, she pushed through the beaded curtain and disappeared into the booth. Elspeth sniffed her disapproval.

There was no immediate demand for Madame Za-Za's services; and, after hanging about for ten minutes or so, Buzz asked Elspeth if he could have a quick look round the Fayre.

'Very well,' she agreed. 'But don't be long.'

The crowds were growing by the minute, and the Fayre's success financially seemed assured. Over the tannoy, owners of dogs being entered for the Show were instructed to take them to the pens at the south end of the field where they would be registered. The Children's Fancy Dress Parade, it was announced, would begin in half-an-hour.

Meanwhile, Fingers' gang had arrived after a fairly uneventful journey. If Fingers cut a somewhat singular figure, people, on the whole, were too polite to stare. One man, on catching sight of the little nurse, did say out loud that he wouldn't like that to be the first face he saw when he came out of anaesthetic. But Fingers pretended that he hadn't heard, and the others, diplomatically, were deaf to the insensitive remark. Inside the school gates, Fingers gave his instructions.

'Right, we'll split up. You all know wot we're lookin' for.'

'Wot's that?' Toe-Rag asked.

'*Buzz's sister*! ... *the bird wot stopped us gettin' the stone back yesterday*! – oh, blimey!' Fingers forced himself to stay cool. 'Now, if ya see 'er, ya don't do nuffin'. Ya find *me* ... right? An', if we ain't turned nuffin' up, we'll meet back 'ere ... Well, go on, then! Don't 'ang about!'

His forces scattered, and Fingers himself began a circuit of the stalls ranged along the perimeter of the field. He had not pursued this inspection long before he halted in his tracks and exclaimed: 'Strewth! Auntie Efful!' Had you been able to follow his line of vision, you would have discovered that what he had in view was the board declaring Madame Za-Za's professional availability. Scarcely had the exclamation died on Fingers' lips, than a second followed. 'It's *'er*!' And it was not to Auntie Efful he referred. He ventured nearer, looking intently at his quarry.

Elspeth, quite unconscious of the interest she excited, sat at her table, idly thumbing through a book of tickets. Tickets were plentiful; customers, so far, were few. It was disappointing. Just then, Fingers clapped his hand to his mouth to stifle a third and potentially atomic exclamation. Beneath Elspeth's table he had spied the case. Fortune was surely smiling on him at last. He moved in closer, ready to seize the case should Elspeth for a moment leave it unattended.

There are people who believe in the power of suggestion. They claim that, if you will something hard enough, your thoughts travel to the other person's brain and they think what you want them to. People of this persuasion will claim Elspeth's sudden jumping up and backing away behind the booth, flapping her hands about her head as evidence of thought transference; and there is no doubt that Fingers had been willing her to move with the intensity which might have moved a mountain. But, unless it can be demonstrated that his thoughts were transferred to the wasp from which Elspeth fled, we cannot accept this as proof. Fingers, however, was totally unconcerned with scientific speculation. He saw only a golden opportunity present itself and he moved in to take advantage of it.

Now, I have to admit I know little about astrology. It is held, I believe, that the life-paths of certain individuals are destined to cross. And, if that is so, I do wonder if the stars under which Mr Voules and Fingers were born fated the one to be the stumbling-block of the other. But the fact is that, even as Fingers was again within inches of his goal, so, for the second time that day, he was thwarted by Mr Voules's intervention.

'Now then, little girl, you're needed in the arena.

The Fancy Dress Parade will be starting very shortly.'

For Mr Voules, dedicated to the service of Mrs Tyte-Knightley, nothing was too trivial which might promote the success of her enterprises. And so it was that he found nothing demeaning in shepherding errant firemen, pirates, pixies and, now, a little nurse to the venue of the Fancy Dress Parade. On hearing that voice, Fingers froze in panic. And it was only when Mr Voules spoke again, that Fingers realised his disguise had not been penetrated. 'You come along with me, young lady.'

Mr Voules's hand clamped on his shoulder, and Fingers found himself being marched to the arena. He wanted to protest, but he dared not speak a word for fear his accents might stir recognition in Mr Voules's memory. And so he attempted to smile winsomely at passers-by who stared at the unlikely pair.

Buzz in his wanderings came to where gathering crowds suggested that something was about to happen. The music had been changed, and now, to the strains of 'The Teddy Bears' Picnic', a straggling line of children in assorted costumes began a circuit of the arena. Mostly they were very small children, and some had to be restrained from running off into the spectators where relatives were waving to them. One of the larger entrants was dressed up as a nurse. She was a conspicuously ungainly girl, and the matchstick thinness of her legs was emphasised by the heavy boots in which she shambled round.

It was to these boots that Buzz found his eyes were drawn. They were boots, he felt, he had beheld before. His gaze travelled upwards and reached the ringleted head at the very moment that the little nurse raised eyes hitherto downcast. And those eyes, dark with passion, glared directly into Buzz's eyes. Buzz clutched the rope which cordoned off the arena. Was it possible? He'd heard of sex-changes – but not within a matter of a few hours, surely? And yet, if Fingers were to be a girl, this is what he'd look like. But *why* should Fingers want to change his gender? He did not seem very happy with the alterations.

The procession passed by; and, shortly after, the winners were announced: a spaceman, a ladybird, and a Donald Duck. Of the nurse there was no mention. And nurse and boots vanished into the crowds. Still feeling a bit shaken by the female-Fingers apparition, Buzz found his way back to Elspeth. Business was picking up, and several clients waited for an audience with Madame Za-Za.

'We're doing quite well now,' Elspeth told Buzz. 'I've already transferred thirty pounds to your case. It soon mounts up. So I'm glad you're back. You can keep a close eye on the money, while I concentrate on the public.'

Lucky old public! thought Buzz, but he sat down without argument at Elspeth's feet. Inside her booth, Madame Za-Za wound up a consultation.

'Yes . . . I definitely see a visitor . . . from the west. Anytime in the next three months you can expect him. That'll be nice for you, won't it, dearie? . . . Well, there's nothing else in the cards today, so we'll leave it there.'

The client returned to the outside world, searching her memory for friends or family who lived 'in the west'; while, left on her own for a few moments, Madame Za-Za fished a green bottle from her skirts to refresh herself. She was mid-swig when the calling of her unprofessional name arrested her.

'*Auntie Efful!* . . . *Auntie Efful!*'

Madame Za-Za dismissed the notion that the green bottle had anything to do with this disembodied voice – after all, a drop of what you fancies never done no one any harm – and she looked about her. Again the voice addressed her.

'*Auntie Efful!*'

So, in her best seance voice, she called back: 'Is there anybody there?'

'*It's me, Auntie!* . . . *Fingers!*'

'Fingers!' cried his relative. 'Fingers, where are ya, ducks?'

'Down 'ere, Auntie.'

Madame Za-Za looked round to see a little nurse

with blonde ringlets scramble beneath the canvas of her booth.

'Fingers? . . . That ain't never you?' she exclaimed in disbelief. 'Oh, Fingers, you ain't turned funny, 'ave you, love?'

Fingers was indignant. 'No! 'Course not! I'm in disguise.'

'Well, thank gawd for that!' said Madame Za-Za, piously. 'So what's all this about then?'

'It's a long story,' Fingers told her. 'An' I'm gonna need yer 'elp.'

''Ang on,' said Madame Za-Za. She stuck her head through the beaded curtain and called to Elspeth. 'Just 'avin' five minutes' break, dearie. It's the strain, you see.' And for the benefit of the queue of clients she added the assurance, 'Just *five* minutes . . . no more!' She returned to Fingers, who faced her across the little green baize table. 'Right,' she said. 'Let's be 'avin' it!'

10

Quick Change Artist

With words few and simple, Fingers put Auntie Efful in the picture; and another generous mouthful from the green bottle enabled the lady to follow his explanation with a steady mind. Then, brushing the back of her hand across her lips, she said: 'O' course I'd 'eard about our Terry skippin' gaol, but I didn't know about 'is little nest-egg ... An' now you're tellin' me there's a quarter of a million sittin' in some kid's school bag outside? – Strewth!' She took one last pull at the green bottle to calm her nerves and then got down to business.

While this conference was in session, clients who had already purchased tickets for Madame Za-Za's services were getting restless. A glance at her watch told Elspeth that the promised five minutes was already close to ten, and she took it on herself to approach the beaded curtain and to call: 'Oh, Madame Za-Za, are you ready now?' From within, she thought she heard the sound of hurried movement, and then Madame Za-Za called back: 'Just 'alf-a-mo, dearie! ... Right, you can ask the next client to step in now.'

When that client emerged from the booth, her

seventy-year-old head reeling with promises of a
romantic encounter across the water, Madame Za-
Za again put her head through the beaded curtain
and called to Buzz.

'Oh, Sonny-Jim! Come 'ere a minute, ducks! . . .
I'm that thirsty! Be a love, will ya, an' go an' buy
me a can of drink – don't matter what kind – and
get one for yerself an' the young lady, too.' She
thrust a five-pound note into Buzz's hand, and he
set off for the refreshment kiosk, which was at the
other side of the field.

Madame Za-Za's next client felt she had scarcely
had her money's worth when the consultation
ended; and, as she left, Madame Za-Za again summoned Elspeth.

'I think my watch 'as stopped,' she said. 'What
time do you make it, dearie?'

'Just ten-to-three,' said Elspeth.

'Are you sure?' asked Madame Za-Za. But,
before Elspeth could reply, a shout went up.

'*Oi*! What d'you think you're doing? . . . That
ain't yours!'

Elspeth turned to see a little girl in a nurse's
uniform racing away, and in her hand she held
Buzz's case.

'The takings!' Elspeth cried. 'She's stolen all the
takings!'

Always a character of swift decision, Elspeth
made at once to pursue the thief, but she found her

71

arm gripped by Madame Za-Za. Utterly feminine though Madame Za-Za was in matters of coiffure, make-up, dress and gold accessories, the strength of her hand would have put her among the Olympic finalists in Swedish Wrestling.

'Oh, no!' exclaimed Madame Za-Za. 'Oh, surely not! There can't be such wickedness in the world!' And, in her anguish, she clasped Elspeth to her breast.

Buzz, bearing the cans of fizzy drink and Madame Za-Za's change, returned just in time to see the Fingers-Nurse figure fleeing through the crowds, and Madame Za-Za, eyes rolled up to heaven, hugging Elspeth to her for comfort in this hour of trial. Elspeth, when she saw her brother staring goggle-eyed at the touching spectacle, managed to gasp from beneath the overhang of Madame Za-Za's bosom: 'The nurse! . . . Stolen your case with all the money!' And then, because Buzz did not have her gift for unhesitating response in an emergency, she snapped: 'Don't just stand there like a goldfish! . . . Get after her!' (Goldfish, of course, do not *stand*; but Elspeth did not have time to polish up her similes.)

'Oh, right!' said Buzz. 'Of course . . . I'll leave the drinks and the change on the table, shall I?'

'*Bother* the drinks!' cried Elspeth, resorting to strong language.

'Yeah . . . right! . . . right!' said Buzz. And, having

72

put the cans and the money down carefully, he devoted his energies to the recovery of the stolen takings. That is to say, he loped off in the direction he had last seen the thief heading, his eyes peeled for anything in a nurse's uniform.

The delay may have been no more than half-a-minute, but it was long enough for a fugitive with the practised skills of Fingers to make good his escape. Having eluded all pursuit, he rested, panting in the lee of a caravan parked in a distant corner of the field. Quickly, he reviewed the state of play. One advantage of being in disguise is that when you have shed the disguise you are virtually disguised again. That is to say, anyone on the lookout for a curly-headed nurse is going to take little notice of a shaven-headed boy in a T-shirt and boxershorts. Now, Fingers was as modest as the next youth and, normally, he would have shrunk from appearing before the public in his underwear. But circumstances were far from normal; and also, he argued, what he was wearing was really little different from athletic gear. He was glad that his favourite pair of boxer-shorts – the ones with hearts and saucy invitations printed on them – were in the wash. There was a sporting chance that he would not attract attention. Speedily, he took off the uniform and wig and stuffed them out of sight beneath the caravan. Then he unzipped the side-pocket of Buzz's case and fished out Cousin Terry's stone.

Toe-Rag was right: it did not look as you would expect a diamond to. It was more like those bits of glass you find on the beach, all the sharp edges worn smooth and their shininess dulled. Fingers kissed it – a mark of affection shown only to items in the highest price range – and then he slipped the gem into the little buttoned pocket of his boxer-shorts.

Costumed as he was, he decided that jogging would help to establish his new role as an athlete; and so he began to trot purposefully in the direction of the gates. Another minute or two and he would be out of the school grounds and winging back to Cousin Terry – mission accomplished! But Luck was fickle. No sooner had she set him scampering joyfully up the winning ladder than he was tumbling back down a dirty great big snake. His discarding of the nurse's uniform and wig was pure plus when it came to escaping the notice of people on the lookout for nurses; but it was one mighty minus when trying to evade anyone with eyes skinned for the familiar features and close-cropped scalp of Fingers Valentine.

A casual observer might have puzzled over why the young sportsman in athletic strip was wearing Doc Martens instead of running-shoes, but he would certainly have asked himself why the booted youth stopped dead in his tracks, turned and sped away as though trying to improve his best time for the hundred metres. Fingers could have told him that it was because he had caught sight of Mr Voules just a split second before Mr Voules's searching optics homed in on him.

Those who had known Mr Voules in the days of his youth had remarked that, while not a team player of distinction, he was, nevertheless, capable of a good turn of speed in track events. And now, despite the rolling years, Mr Voules demonstrated that he could still leg it with the best. His lower limbs were a blur as relentlessly he followed in pursuit. A glance over his shoulder showed Fingers that Mr Voules, like an avenging Fury, was hard upon his heels; and, in desperation, he leapt over an obstructing rope to find himself, once more, in the arena.

11

A Clash of Cultures

The first time Fingers was there, you will recall, it was as a competitor in the Fancy Dress Parade. On this, his second appearance, again he was not alone. Some two dozen youths in athletic vests and shorts were assembling in the middle of the field, and Fingers flung himself into their midst for cover.

Mr Voules, in the excitement of the chase, likewise attempted to vault the rope which separated spectators from performers, but he was unlucky enough to catch his toe on it and to fall headlong on the grass. This accident and the sniggers which greeted his misfortune did not sweeten him. He scrambled to his feet and stormed across the field to the boys who were forming into rows. Among this disciplined body of Marie Lloyd's outstanding gymnasts Fingers was attempting to conceal himself.

'Valentine!' bawled Mr Voules, the foam flying from his lips. 'Come here, you miserable little toad!'

But Fingers was not to be coaxed out like that; and Mr Voules began pulling and pushing boys aside, thus disturbing the neat symmetry of their formation. This was the moment when Mr Voules heard himself addressed in a style to which he was not accustomed.

'What the *something something* do y'think y' *something* doin'?'

Why, Cousin Terry! you exclaim. And, having only cold print to inform you, it is not an unintelligent conclusion. But, if you had heard the accent made familiar by Australian TV soaps, you would have realised that, though the vocabulary and sentiments were those of Cousin Terry, the tongue which uttered them was Antipodean. In fact, the burly individual in the designer track-suit who had had the temerity to question Mr Voules in these immoderate terms was none other than Mad Max himself. At the best of times Mad Max was low on tolerance; but now, just when he hoped to bask in thunderous applause as his crack squad demonstrated what a bit of good old Aussie coaching could achieve, this Pommie creep was pushing his lads around. Well, cobber, *two* could play at that game! So, eye-balling Mr Voules and jabbing a karate tensioned forefinger into Mr Voules's wishbone, he repeated his enquiry.

Staggering backwards, Mr Voules was distracted from the quest for Fingers. The crimson mist before his eyes cleared sufficiently for him to recognise in his assailant the deranged colonial – no doubt of convict stock – whom Mrs Tyte-Knightley, in a rare lapse from sound judgement, had appointed on a one year's contract. If Mr Voules had any say in it, that contract would not be renewed. But Mad Max, who found himself in flattering demand with the local 'Sheilas', was in no hurry to start searching the 'wanted' ads in *The Times Educational Supplement*. And success with today's display would, he reckoned, clinch his reappointment. Thus, that afternoon, he had quite as much at stake as Mr Voules, whom, in any case, he didn't like – whom, in fact, he particularly disliked. For he knew instinctively that Mr Voules was just the kind of pervert who would rather have his beer poured into a glass than drink it from a can.

'Mr Maxwell!' said Mr Voules, frostily.

Mad Max's eyes narrowed with suspicion and contempt. He never trusted these guys with their plummy voices and their 'Misters'. And, if this prize prune thought he was going to put one over a red-blooded boy from Oz, then he could *something* think again.

'Mr Maxwell,' Mr Voules repeated, 'there is a boy here whom I must take with me.'

That clinched it for Mad Max. In his experience, anyone who said 'whom' was up to something fishy; so . . . 'Get knotted, Voules!' he said.

'*Mr Maxwell*!'

'Oh . . . take a runnin' jump!'

'Mr Maxwell, I am warning you!'

This was a challenge – a challenge which the honour of the house of Maxwell could not ignore.

'Oh, yeah!' Mad Max snarled. And he shoved Mr

Voules with the barrel of his out-thrust chest. It was like being butted by a Sherman tank.

'Mr Maxwell!' protested Mr Voules.

'Oh, yeah!' again Mad Max wittily replied. And again he chested Mr Voules.

From the gymnastic squad a cheer went up. And Mr Voules, taking to heart the maxim that discretion is the better part of valour, retreated and contented himself by promising Mad Max, from a safe distance, that he had not heard the last of this.

While this entertaining episode claimed everyone's attention, Fingers seized the opportunity to slip away, out of the limelight, to where he could lose himself in the crowds once more. But he was a marked man. He knew it. At any moment, he might be caught, and he could not risk being taken with the stone in his possession. It was imperative to find another place for its concealment. How he wished it was still in the comparative safety of Buzz's bag. Even as he wrestled with the problem, his head turned this way and that like a bird which keeps a watchful eye for moggies. And his caution was justified by a sighting of Mr Voules, systematically trawling the playing field for him and fast approaching.

Fingers happened, at that moment, to be in the area reserved for the Dog Show. Here were dogs sleeping, dogs scratching, dogs exploring themselves, dogs trying to explore other dogs. And, on an upturned box stood a silver cup and an opened tin of dog food. With no time to weigh up advantages and disadvantages, Fingers took the diamond from his pocket and poked it deep into the dog food. As soon as Mr Voules had passed, he would return and retrieve the stone. Now, you and I, with time to evaluate the pros and cons of this scheme, can see at least as many cons as pros. But time was what Fingers did not have. Action was demanded of him then and there. And so he pushed the jewel deep into the can of Rover's Relish, and made off.

12

A Dog's Dinner

Meanwhile, what of Buzz? – For Mr Voules was not the only one who sought the elusive Fingers. Mr Voules, as we have seen, had come within a whisker of success only to be foiled by the unseemly set-to with Mad Max. And, while this high drama was being enacted centre-stage in the arena, Buzz trotted to and fro like a baffled fox-hound. But he caught no glimpse of nurses great or small, blonde or brunette, with bags or without. He knew that his returning to Elspeth empty-handed would be rewarded with a bruising lecture on his uselessness in general and in the tracking down of takings-takers in particular. And so, although he had abandoned any hope of catching Fingers, he continued going through the motions of a search if only to delay reporting back. At length weary and dejected, he came upon a corner of the field which held little interest for your average pleasure seeker, and he decided to devote a minute to rest and recollection in the shelter of a caravan which was standing there.

Buzz sank onto the grass, leant his back against the caravan, and mused. And the conclusion of his musings was that Life was a funny old business.

It just would not leave a boy alone. He sighed and decided to count to twenty before going back to face the music. He counted slowly, the way he did to put off getting out of bed: 'One . . . two . . . three . . .' until he came to 'eighteen . . . nineteen . . . nineteen-and-a-half. . . nineteen-and-threequarters . . . nineteen-and-seven-eighths . . .' His grasp of vulgar fractions was at its limit, and, at last, with a heavy heart, he pronounced the 'twenty'.

It was as he struggled to his feet that he noticed there was something underneath the caravan – in fact, several somethings. With mounting excitement, Buzz pulled them out: a blonde, curly wig; a nurse's uniform and cap; and . . . *his case*! It was fastened, but it would be too much to hope that the money was still inside. Nevertheless, he opened it and looked. And the cash was there! Now why should the thief – Fingers, of course – make good his getaway and leave the cash behind? But the main thing was he'd got the money back. That would be one in the eye for Elspeth. For the first time in days, Buzz chuckled. He resisted the temptation to gallop back to Madame Za-Za's booth, exclaiming: 'I've got it! I've got it!' Instead, he sauntered. And, when he got to Elspeth, he put the case down on the table, saying, 'I've not counted it, but I think you'll find it's all there . . . Oh, I'll have that drink now.'

As Buzz lifted the can to his lips, he watched Elspeth from the corner of his eye. Her face was, as they say, a picture. The offering of compliments did not come easily to her.

'Oh . . . you've got it back!' she said, and opened the bag. 'Yes . . . yes, it's all here. Er . . . well done, Richard.'

'You're welcome,' Buzz replied.

'There ain't nothing missin', then?' asked Madame Za-Za.

'No,' Buzz assured her. 'The side pocket's open, but I never keep anything in there.'

'That's all right, then,' said Madame Za-Za, sighing with relief. 'And you never caught no one?'

'No,' said Buzz. 'But I think I know who it was.'

Madame Za-Za felt a spasm of alarm.

'I found a wig,' Buzz explained, 'and a nurse's uniform. I think it was a boy called . . .' Buzz stopped himself. He didn't want to get involved again with Fingers. They'd got the money, so best leave it there.

'Well, back to business, eh?' said Madame Za-Za briskly. 'I knew something like this was goin' to 'appen . . . In the tea leaves it was this mornin' . . . Right, next please!' she called and vanished into the dim sanctuary behind the beaded curtain.

Buzz was determined to make the most of having the moral advantage over Elspeth, and he told her – *told* not *asked* – that he was going to have another stroll about the Fayre. Elspeth was not pleased by this show of independence; but her debt to him was great, and the sooner she had paid it off, the sooner she could start bossing him again.

The public address system informed the crowds that the judging of the Dog Show was in progress; so Buzz bent his steps in that direction. He was not knowledgeable on the subject of dogs. He could distinguish between your big dog and your small dog; and he knew that some dogs were disposed to bite your legs. But as to the finer points which judges looked for, he hadn't a clue. He watched now as owners paraded their dogs and made them stand and sit. He observed the judges as they ran their hands over canine frames and peered inside jaws to count the teeth. Then the winners of the various classes were announced, and finally the Supreme Champion.

'Britannia's Glory, owned by Miss Jocasta Ewebank!'

Buzz looked on as the Champion was led forward. Now, it is often claimed that beauty is in the eye of the beholder. But, as Buzz beheld Britannia's Glory, he decided it was not in the eye of just any old beholder. In the case of Britannia's Glory, it was not in Buzz's eye.

Britannia's Glory was one of the bulldog breed. He had jaws and fangs resembling a man-trap; a nose pushed back so far that breathing was accomplished in snorts and grunts; a low brow furrowed with the effort of thought; eyes which bulged with primitive emotion; and short, bandy legs. And the sum total of these deformities, it seemed, was beauty.

'And now,' said the announcer, 'Mr Cyril Wellbeloved of our sponsors will present the cup to Miss Ewebank and a well-earned tin of Rover's Relish to Britannia's Glory!'

A procession, comprising a short, stout man in a loud, check suit, followed by two kennelmaids carrying the trophy and a tin of dog food, advanced to the winner's podium. Miss Ewebank took possession of the cup, and the tin of Rover's Relish was emptied into a bowl and presented to the star himself. Britannia's Glory was not a dainty eater. Just three gulps and the dish was emptied. This dispatch of the Rover's Relish amid the flashing of cameras was greeted with applause; and then Miss Ewebank led the Champion in a victor's circuit.

It was while Britannia's Glory was snuffling and waddling along at Miss Ewebank's brogue-shod heels that *it* struck home at his doggy heart. Not the same *it* which Mrs Tyte-Knightley and Elspeth boasted. This was quite another *it*. In playground discussions of what-made-the-world-go-round, a commonplace was that either you had *it* or you had not. And Buzz had decided that as far as Tracy Welstead was concerned – who had *it* and enough to spare! – he had none at all, or, at any rate, not enough to make a difference. But, if Tracy Welstead found him wanting in animal magnetism, so did not Britannia's Glory.

Critics who wish to belittle Buzz's success with the Show Champion will say that any dog which can hog a tin of Rover's Relish must be a dog with simple tastes. Be that as it may, the fact is that, just as the creature was passing Buzz in its triumphal progress, it suddenly sat down on its hunkers, its nostrils sucking in deep draughts of something special, and its eyes fixed on Buzz with longing and devotion.

'Come on, boy!' Miss Ewebank encouraged him, and jerked his lead. But Britannia's Glory was immovable. He sat there, his whole being transfigured into a poem of adoration.

'Dammit!' exclaimed Miss Ewebank. She identified the object of the bulldog's worship, and again exclaimed: 'Dammit!' Adding, 'You do choose your moments, Snuffles!' Then she addressed herself to Buzz. 'Look here, sonny, d'you mind walking with me? It's the only way we'll get him on the move. He's taken a fancy to you, y'see ... Happens now and then. Don't ask me why. Must be something to do with your smell.'

This was a wounding observation. For some time, Buzz had worried that his lack of success with Tracy Welstead was related to what in advice columns is referred to as 'body odour'; and stowed at the back of a drawer in his bedroom was an impressive collection of deodorants. To be told now that what repelled the object of his erotic dreams was a big turn-on for a dog did nothing for his self-esteem. But Buzz, as we have already seen, found it difficult to say 'no'; and Miss Ewebank was yet another female born into the ranks of women who sweep all before them. Therefore, our hero found himself stumbling along beside the Champion's owner with the Champion himself panting, trance-like, after him.

Well may you feel for Buzz in his embarrassment. But spare some sympathy for Fingers, whose sufferings at that moment were even more acute. For Fingers, too, had witnessed the final moments of the Dog Show. As soon as the coast was clear of Voules, he had returned with the object of retrieving the diamond; and he had arrived just in time to see the tin of dog food being borne away and tipped into the winner's dinner plate; and then to watch Britannia's Glory devour the lot in the twinkling of an eye. This appalling spectacle left even the resourceful Fingers stunned, unable to think, far less to act. And it was only the sudden digging of steely fingers into the skin and muscle tissue of his right shoulder which roused him from his paralytic state. He leapt, convinced that Mr Voules had crept up on him unawares. But the voice which spoke into his ear was not the voice of Mr Voules.

'Where's my *something* diamond, Fingers?' it demanded, hoarsely.

13

A Painful Confession

Cousin Terry had grown impatient. Waiting did not agree with him. Rather than wait for his release from Her Majesty's Prison, he had left prematurely, without giving notice that he was planning to vacate his cell. And, now, he had found it impossible to wait for Fingers to come back with the diamond. For one thing, the kid had brains – the whole family agreed that Fingers was a bright one – and Cousin Terry never really trusted kids with brains. He wouldn't put it past Fingers to leave him (Cousin Terry) sitting in Our Norman's flat, while he (Fingers) caught a plane to South America with his (Cousin Terry's) diamond in his pocket. He kicked himself for getting the little clever-clogs to look after the sparkler in the first place. And so, telling Our Norman that he'd 'ad it up to 'ere! (indicating the level of his Adam's apple), he'd helped himself to his host's trench coat and trilby hat, and, with the collar of the one turned up and the brim of the other turned down, had set off for the Summer Fayre, where, if Fingers were to be believed, he might be found. And, as we learned at the end of Chapter Twelve, his efforts were rewarded.

But the question he put to his young relative was badly timed – from Fingers' point of view. Never had the telling of the truth seemed less inviting. For Fingers could not imagine Cousin Terry, on being informed that his diamond was in a bulldog's stomach, shrugging it off philosophically and saying: 'Well, you win some; you lose some.' No! Philosophy was not Cousin Terry's style ... Grievous bodily harm was more in his line.

'Not 'ere, Terry!' Fingers stammered. 'Not 'ere!'

'Wotcher mean, "not 'ere"?' growled Cousin Terry. 'Where is it then?'

'No, I mean we can't *talk* 'ere.' Fingers squirmed as Cousin Terry's tightening grip threatened to separate his arm from his torso like the wing torn from a roasted chicken at a mediaeval banquet.

'*Why* not 'ere?' demanded Cousin Terry.

'We might be 'eard.'

'I'll risk it.' Cousin Terry lowered his mouth close to Fingers' ear. '*Where ... is ... it?*'

Fingers gulped. 'Look, I can explain.'

'Don't explain ... *Tell* me ... Where is it?'

'Well,' said Fingers, 'you ain't never gonna believe this, Terry.'

'Try me.'

'Well ... see that dog? ... the one walkin' round the ring?'

'Ain't nuffin' wrong wiv me *something* eyes,' said Cousin Terry. 'I can see a dog, but I can't see no *something* diamond.'

'Well . . . it's there,' said Fingers.

'Wotcher mean? . . . Where?'

'There.'

'*Where*?'

Fingers swallowed hard. 'Inside the dog.'

Cousin Terry was slow to take on board any new idea. Once he had got it, it was hard to dislodge; but the initial learning process was laborious.

' "Inside the *dog*",' he repeated, concentrating on the words.

'Yeah,' croaked Fingers.

' "*Inside* the dog",' Cousin Terry said again, varying the emphasis.

'Yeah.'

Cousin Terry paused for contemplation. Then light flooded his understanding.

'Inside the *something* dog!' he roared.

Bystanders turned their heads to observe this wild, coated and behatted figure which cursed beneath the summer sun.

'*Ssh*!' hissed Fingers. 'People are lookin' . . . D'ya want the Old Bill to know yer 'ere?'

'You've got some explainin'!' Cousin Terry snarled. 'An' you'd better make it *something* good!'

'It's complicated,' Fingers told him, 'but I'll cut it short. I got the stone – right? – but then I 'ad to 'ide it in a 'urry. An' the only place was this tin of dog food – right?'

90

Cousin Terry frowned as he tried to follow the sequence of events.

'An' then,' continued Fingers, 'before I could get it back, they fed it to the dog.'

Cousin Terry's grip shifted from Fingers' shoulder to his windpipe.

'No, Terry!' Fingers wheezed. 'No! Not 'ere!'

Even in his emotional state, Cousin Terry could just appreciate that the strangulation of a minor demanded privacy, and he relaxed the pressure which was making Fingers' breathing difficult. And, while Fingers gulped down litres of fresh air, Cousin Terry put matters to him simply.

'*You* got the *something* diamond in the dog. *You* can *something* git it out!'

'Right,' nodded Fingers, who, at that moment, would have agreed to stealing the meat rations from a tiger. The question of 'how?' he was feeding into his mental software even as he witnessed at the other side of the arena the encounter between Britannia's Glory and Buzz Beecham. For throughout the fraught interview with Cousin Terry, Fingers had been mindful of the importance of keeping an eye fixed on the diamond-loaded bulldog. And he watched now, keenly, as Buzz joined the doggy lady, and Britannia's Glory followed in his footsteps.

As Fingers stood there watching, he was joined by Picker, Toe-Rag, and Tiny. The three stared curiously at the menacing form which towered over

Fingers, Toe-Rag began to say: ''Ere, is this yer Cousin Ter . . .?' when Tiny stamped on his foot and then looked up shyly for the great man's approval. He felt he had handled Toe-Rag's indiscretion in true Cousin Terry manner; but Cousin Terry ignored his youthful fan, only muttering to Fingers: 'You'll find me in the beer tent when you've got it. An' you'd better get it *something* quick! . . . Right?'

'Right,' said Fingers.

When Cousin Terry had left them to themselves, Picker asked: ''Ow d'ya get on, Fingers? . . . An' wot ya doin' in yer pants?'

Briefly, Fingers gave them an update on the situation.

'Blimey!' Tiny whistled. ''Ow the 'ell d'ya get a diamond out of a bulldog?'

And that – as Hamlet observed about another knotty problem – was the question.

Britannia's Glory had completed his lap of honour and, in the company of Buzz and Miss Ewebank, was entering the winner's enclosure. Fingers and his accomplices drifted in the same direction while they searched the attics of their minds for the makings of a plan.

'We could cut it open,' suggested Tiny.

'An' I suppose you think the brute'll just lie on its back an' let ya do it!' said Fingers scornfully.

It was Toe-Rag who again came up with the solution.

'Our Sharon swallowed Mum's engagement ring when she was a baby.'

'Don't tell me!' Picker sneered. 'You cut 'er open with the breadknife!'

'No,' said Toe-Rag. 'I don't fink Mum thought of that . . . No, she jus' sort of waited.'

'Waited?' said Tiny.

'Yeah, waited . . . You know.'

'You mean until she . . .?' Picker said.

'Yeah,' said Toe-Rag.

'And then you 'ad to . . .?'

'Yeah.'

'Ugh! . . . That's gross!'

'Yeah,' Toe-Rag said. 'But Mum got 'er ring back.'

Fingers and his confederates pondered the moral of Toe-Rag's story. In seeking to recover the diamond from the dark interior of Britannia's Glory, Nature was on their side. But Nature was going to demand her price for the safe delivery of the stone – a price no one fancied paying. And there was the question of time. Just how long did it take for an uncut diamond to travel the entire length of the internal workings of a bulldog? And, no less, there was the question of accessibility. It was one thing for Toe-Rag's mum to monitor the bowel movements of her infant daughter; it was quite another to find the opportunity of examining the deposits of a total stranger's champion bulldog.

Fingers wrestled with the problem and reduced

it to its basic elements. They were: (1) that, if he did not get the diamond back to Cousin Terry, Cousin Terry's face would be the last he saw in this world; and (2) that being so, any risks entailed in recovering the diamond were to be preferred. On the basis of this analysis, he came to his decision.

'Dogs do poo every day, don't they?' he said.

'Oh, yeah,' said Picker. 'My Uncle Tony's got this alsatian in 'is backyard, an' they're always shovellin' it up.'

'So,' continued Fingers, 'twenty-four hours should see the diamond through?'

'I'd say so,' Picker said, who, on the strength of his Uncle Tony, spoke with authority.

'Prunes might 'urry things along,' Toe-Rag suggested.

Fingers opened his mouth to answer, but shook his head and concentrated on what mattered.

'Then we've got to get 'old of that dog for twenty-four hours, or for as long as it takes to come up with the goods,' he said.

The others stared at him in disbelief.

'Ya don't mean *kidnap* it?' said Tiny.

'Yeah,' Fingers said defiantly. 'That's exactly wot I do mean!'

14

Punch-Up!

'You've made a hit with Snuffles, right enough,' Miss Ewebank said. 'The great big softy!'

The bulldog was sitting at Buzz's feet and gazed up at him with deep emotion. Buzz reached down and scratched the animal between the ears. This gesture of affection overwhelmed Britannia's Glory, and he rolled over on his back, his tongue lolling out in ecstasy.

'Oh, pat his tummy, for goodness' sake!' Miss Ewebank ordered Buzz.

Buzz stooped and commenced the patting. In an effort to make conversation, he said, 'I suppose he's quite valuable.'

'Could have got five hundred for him yesterday,' replied Miss Ewebank. 'But he'll be worth a bit more than that to some people now.' Little she knew how true she spoke. 'Not that I'd part with him for a fortune... Now, look here, sonny,' she went on, 'I need to go and powder m'nose. Do you think you could hang on here for a couple of minutes and keep the dozy bugger company?' And, before Buzz could excuse himself from dogminding duties, she was gone.

Buzz was still kneeling and patting when a goose-pimply sensation in the back of his neck informed him that he was not alone. Buzz abandoned the patting and looked round to find Fingers standing there, flanked by Tiny, Picker and Toe-Rag, who tried to hide the fact that their leader was still clad in just his boxer-shorts, singlet and Doc Martens. Fingers had kept Buzz and Miss Ewebank in his sights, and, seeing the lady stride purposefully away in the direction of the 'Ladies', he calculated he had just a few minutes in which to abduct her dog. And, as Britannia's Glory lay there on his back, snorting with delight as his ribs were tickled, he seemed to present no threat. That left only Buzz to deal with. Forthwith, Fingers rapidly devised a plan; a few hasty words to his accomplices; and then it was action-stations and *go, go, go!*

'Someone wants ya, Buzz,' said Fingers. 'Tiny'll show ya where. Better 'urry up.'

'Er, who wants me?' Buzz asked suspiciously.

''E said "'urry up"!' Tiny threatened, and he seized Buzz by the arm. This was a mistake, for Britannia's Glory was fiercely loyal to those he loved. In an instant, the bulldog was on his feet, snarling deep and menacingly, and displaying teeth which gave Tiny food for thought.

'Nice doggy, nice doggy!' Tiny said, and let go of Buzz's arm.

Fingers' brain came close to melt-down as he

tried to adjust to this new situation. Buzz could not be separated from the dog. Therefore, where the dog went Buzz must also go – or, rather, where Buzz went the dog, like Mary's little lamb, was sure to follow. How then to persuade Buzz to accompany them without any display of physical force which would antagonise the animal? The answer lay in psychology. What would a *nice* boy like Buzz most dread? . . . Trouble with authority. For Fingers and his tribe, authority and trouble were inseparable; it was a way of life. But not for the Buzzes of this world.

'I fink you should come wiv us, Buzz, me old mate,' said Fingers.

'Why?'

"Cos I gather old Tyte-Knightley is still dead keen to find out who got thrown off the bus the other day an' acted so disgraceful.'

'But . . . but I never!' Buzz stammered.

'Maybe. But "no smoke wivout fire". That's wot old T-K is gonna say when a little bird sings your name.'

'Well . . . where are we going?' Buzz asked in despair. 'What do you want me for?'

'Don't ask questions. Jus' trust me.'

'Trust *you*!'

'Look,' Fingers said, 'I'll level wiv ya. Ain't no one gonna get 'urt nor nuffin'. But, if ya don't come *now*, it might be anuvver story. *And* you'll 'ave old

Tyte-Knightley after ya.'

Buzz was no hero. His was not the stuff which cries: 'Villain, do your worst! One here will stand true what'er the cost!' But he did say: 'What about that dog? I'm supposed to take care of it.'

'Bring it wiv ya.'

'But . . .'

'You 'eard 'im,' said Tiny, while keeping a wary eye on the business end of Britannia's Glory.

'Oh . . . all right,' Buzz said.

'Good! Come on!' said Fingers, and he took the first step towards the exit, which lay at the far end of the field.

Feeling like the victim in a gangster movie who is hustled to a waiting car with a gun prodding him in the back, Buzz walked ahead with Fingers. Britannia's Glory padded loyally along at Buzz's heels, and the others again fell into a protective phalanx.

Thought Fingers: So far, so good. Once we're out of 'ere, we'll take the dog to Our Norman's and keep it there until we can get our 'ands on the diamond. (He hoped it would not be *his* hands.) But they would have to dump Buzz somewhere on the way so that he didn't know where they were going. Fingers looked back thoughtfully at Britannia's Glory. How to separate him from Buzz? He could only hope that something would turn up. But the lucky breaks were not with Fingers Valentine that day.

As boys and bulldog threaded their way through the crowds, the programme of entertainments was coming to its climax, and into the arena marched first the Salvation Army Band, playing 'Get Me to the Church on Time', followed by the Mile End Majorettes. Majorettes are not everybody's cup of tea. But, like them or not, you have to admit they are very skilful with their twirlers. And the girls of the Mile End Majorettes were second to none when it came to twirling. Their batons spun high and low, now above their heads, now behind their backs, now from hand to hand. And, all the while, the Majorettes marched with a brisk thigh-flashing action. It was very impressive. If you have the taste for that sort of thing.

Out at the front, marching on her own and leading the way, was Sandra Plunkett. At home, the Plunkett sideboard was crowded with trophies Sandra had won for twirling. She had even been in the team which had twirled for Britain, and the Mile End band was justly proud of her. That day, she was on form; and, as she marched with head high, she tossed her baton spinning skywards and deftly caught it as it fell. It's difficult to remain modest when you know you are the best, and Sandra was but human. And, so, egged on by the gasps and plaudits of the crowd, Sandra tossed her baton ever higher.

Now that you have this picture of the Sally Army with their gleaming instruments parading to a sprightly four-four melody, followed by the Majorettes with their high-knee marching and their twirling batons, it but remains to explain that Fingers, Buzz, Britannia's Glory and the others were passing close to the arena just where there was a gap in the assembled spectators, and just as Sandra was beginning an about-turn to lead the Majorettes back up the field in the footsteps of the band. Tossing a baton high into the air while you are executing an about-turn is difficult and, perhaps, Sandra should not have attempted it. As it was, her judgement was just that tiny fraction out, and she experienced every twirler's nightmare... She dropped her baton! It happens; and the public is forgiving. The thing to do is to pick the baton up and continue the routine. But, on this occasion, the gods who punish pride in vainglorious mortals had it in for Sandra.

If Britannia's Glory were to appear in a dogs' *Who's Who*, he would list under 'pastimes': barking at cats and chasing sticks. And so, when he saw Sandra's baton fall to the ground a few feet from him, he did what a dog does. With a joyful bark, he leapt forward to take possession of the baton. He was in a playful mood, and the bark, I repeat, was an expression of the joy of living. But to appreciate that you would need to know him very well. What Sandra and her cohorts heard was a deep-throated roar which would have not disgraced the Hound of the Baskervilles. And what they saw was a slavering beast with bared fangs bounding towards them. Their screams drowned the Salvation Army's rendition of 'The Dam-Busters' Theme', and batons rained to the earth like another plague on Egypt. Majorettes at the back marched into Majorettes at the front, and Majorettes fell over.

Now, Britannia's Glory only ever had room in his head for one idea at a time; and, undistracted by the pandemonium, he seized Sandra's baton and ran off into the middle of the field. Fingers, too, had only one idea: at whatever cost he must not lose that dog. And so, abandoning all caution, he chased after Britannia's Glory.

The uproar attracted general attention, and among those drawn to the source of the disturbance was Mr Voules. He was still prowling the field in search of Fingers and, when he saw his quarry in pursuit of a bulldog, he too gave chase. It says much for his general fitness that he caught up with Fingers and seized him by a skinny arm.

'Gotcher!' he exclaimed in triumph.

Fingers squealed and wriggled, desperate to escape as he watched Britannia's Glory growing ever smaller in the distance.

'Lemme go! Lemme go, ya big baboon!' he shouted; and he kicked Mr Voules in the shins. He kicked him hard.

At this point, passion got the better of Mr Voules's reason. He *knew*, no matter how great the provocation, it was a crime to strike a pupil. He *knew* the Valentines could sue him for assault. Nevertheless, with his free hand he belted Fingers round the ear. Most people, regardless of the legal niceties, rather sympathised with Mr Voules. But not everyone. Cousin Terry didn't.

He had had enough of sitting in the beer tent, and he, too, had come seeking Fingers; and his feelings towards his junior relative were still on the wrong side of murderous. But blood is thicker than water, and it was quite another thing for an outsider to land the little weasel one. Thus it was that Cousin Terry's family loyalty was his undoing. As an escaped convict, he should have shunned publicity. He should not have indulged in punch-ups before a multitude of witnesses. But, with a roar which outdid any effort of Britannia's Glory, he charged into the middle of the field and swung Mr Voules round to face him, and, in words which had a familiar ring in the ears of the schoolmaster, he demanded: 'Wot the *something something* do ya fink yer *something* doin'?' And then, not waiting for an answer, he punched Mr Voules on the nose.

Taken aback by this, Mr Voules let go of Fingers; and, when he saw a bloodied fist drawn back for another blow, he instinctively got his in first – below the belt. Cousin Terry doubled up, gasping oaths too terrible even for the use of asterisks.

It says little for the depraved tastes of the general public that this spectacle was proving to be the highlight of the afternoon; and the combatants were being urged on with shouts of encouragement and advice. Neither was needed. Cousin Terry fought with the instinct of a pit bull terrier, and Mr Voules with the desperation of a man who struggles for his life. The odds among those who were already laying bets on the outcome of the duel favoured Cousin Terry. But this was before a third contender joined the fray.

Among the onlookers attracted by the hullabaloo was Mrs Tyte-Knightley. She had been conducting local dignitaries about the Fayre, and, until that moment, it had been a successful exercise in public relations. But now she stood aghast as she watched her Deputy engaged, tooth and nail, in a brawl of unrestrained ferocity. Something had to be done, and done quickly. Among her entourage was Mad Max, who had been congratulated on the excellence of his gymnastics team. To him Mrs Tyte-Knightley turned. What was called for now, she knew, was muscle. And what Mad Max lacked in intellect he made up for with his biceps.

'Mr Maxwell,' Mrs Tyte-Knightley said, '*do* something!' She should have known that she was pouring petrol on the flames.

Mad Max had not enjoyed a proper punch-up

since he and his mates had wrecked the bar on his last night in Kalgoorlie. His natural sympathies lay with Cousin Terry, because anyone who was knocking the living daylights out of Voules must have decent values. But, to make the most of a punch-up, you had to put prejudice aside and thump everyone impartially. And it was with this even-handed approach that he threw himself into the conflict. Like Cousin Terry, he did aim his first blow at Mr Voules's nose – for it is not only great minds which think alike – but then he drove his knee into Cousin Terry's groin. The two Englishmen, knowing only that they were assaulted by a third and uninvited party, flung themselves at their new assailant in a tangle of threshing arms and legs.

For some punch-ups are definitely a spectator sport. They will pay for a seat at the ring-side, or they will buy a TV licence and, in the comfort of their homes, will watch the Hooded Horror head-butt the Kilburn Killer. And this satisfies them. But, for others, secondhand experience is not enough. And that is why so many young men, seeing Mad Max join the action, took this as a signal that it was a free-for-all. One after the other, they sprang from the ranks of passive bystanders and pitched in.

How long this disgraceful scene continued Mrs Tyte-Knightley could never say. But long enough for the press photographers to get some juicy pictures for the late editions; long enough for the owner of a camcorder to shoot the proceedings and sell his film to the local TV station; and long enough for the police to be summoned and for half-a-dozen squad cars with flashing lights and screaming sirens to arrive. The Great Marie Lloyd Riot was national news. Bishops made statements. Questions were asked in Parliament. But this is the public side of the affair, and our concern is with the private fortunes of the individuals whose history we have followed.

Fingers, ever resourceful and single-minded, as soon as Mr Voules lost interest in him, sped after Britannia's Glory. He still had hopes of recovering Cousin Terry's diamond. With inviting cries of ''Ere, boy!' he pursued the animal as it gambolled about the field, still carrying Sandra's baton in its jaws. But Fingers did not have whatever it was that Buzz had, and Britannia's Glory paid no heed until another voice rang out: 'Snuffles! Here! Heel!' Miss Ewebank, nose powdered, had perceived her dog, not where she had left it under supervision, but frisking free. She was not best pleased. 'Here!' she repeated in tones which no man or beast would care to disobey. Britannia's Glory knew the game was up. He waddled to his mistress and wagged his stumpy tail ingratiatingly.

'Drop it!' said Miss Ewebank.

Sandra's baton, dripping with dog slobber, fell to the ground, and the Supreme Champion followed meekly to Miss Ewebank's estate car, into the back of which, with help, he climbed and was driven away.

Fingers looked on, speechless and numb with disappointment. He was joined by Toe-Rag and Picker. Tiny was rejoicing in his element as he punched and kicked on the fringes of the battle which raged in the middle of the arena. It was, he felt, good work-experience for a would-be 'heavy'.

The rumpus had so stirred Elspeth's curiosity that she sacrificed some dignity and stood on her chair to see what was going on.

'There's a most terrible fight,' she reported to Madame Za-Za. 'Gracious me! There's Mr Voules in the middle of it! . . . and Mr Maxwell! . . . and an awful looking man in a heavy coat!'

Just then a police siren announced the arrival of the forces of law and order, and Madame Za-Za decided it would be prudent to withdraw.

'Don't think we'll do much more business today, dear,' she said. 'You just give me the takings and I'll be off.'

'Do you mean all of them?' Elspeth asked, uneasily.

'Yes, I'll settle up with the School later . . . Come on, sweetheart! I'm in a 'urry!'

Elspeth opened Buzz's case, and Madame Za-Za transferred the accumulated cash into the deep pockets which lined her skirts. Then, with a breezy,

'Ta-ta, dearie!' she was gone.

And Buzz, watching the scene of chaos and confusion, found he was alone. Fingers he had seen race after Britannia's Glory, and he had watched Tiny hurry to attack the lower limbs of perfect strangers with his boots. But he had not noticed Toe-Rag and Picker melt away. And it was only when policemen with their truncheons charged onto the field that he realised that he was unaccompanied and free. This was the moment, he decided, while Fingers was still occupied and before Miss Ewebank returned, for him to make for home. Elspeth and Madame Za-Za and the takings could all go hang! The last few days had been a nightmare. Something had been going on, but what it was he didn't know, and he did not want to know. All he wanted now was *out*!

Among those eventually arrested was Cousin Terry; and, when he had been identified, the police took credit for the recapture of a dangerous criminal ... the fruits of painstaking detective-work and vigilance. Down at the police station, Cousin Terry kicked and hammered at his cell door, shouting that the *something* dog 'ad got 'is *something* property, and that there weren't no *something* justice. The officer in charge, who was nursing a black eye, told him to shut his *something* face!

15

Epilogue

On Sunday morning, bright and early, while Buzz was still in bed and wondering if he could stay there for a year or two, Miss Ewebank was taking Britannia's Glory for his first walk of the day. They made their usual circuit of the park, and, halfway round, the Supreme Champion squatted to answer Nature's call. Miss Ewebank was, as you would expect, a responsible dog-owner and she carried with her a pooper-scooper for just such eventualities. With it she collected the malodorous deposit and popped it into the nearest bin provided for the purpose. Then she led Britannia's Glory home to breakfast, leaving the park to the birds and bees and flowers.

And to a ferrety-faced youth with a Number One and Doc Martens, who emerged from behind a beech tree. He pulled on a pair of yellow kitchen gloves and, swallowing hard, he lifted the lid of the bin and reached down inside.

Other Titles by Roger Collinson

BUTTERFINGERS

'Could well be the funniest book of the year . . . comic writing of the highest order.' *Times Educational Supplement*
ISBN 0 86264 746 0   hardback

GET LAVINIA GOODBODY!

Illustrated by John Shelley
'Figgy, his family, friends and enemies are woven with great skill into a slick, action-packed and very funny story.' *Junior Bookshelf*
ISBN 0 86264 054 7   hardback

GRISEL AND THE TOOTH FAIRY & Other Stories

Illustrated by Tony Ross
This new collection of short stories features the wayward and spirited Griselda, otherwise known as Grisel. Whether hijacking the school Nativity play with unauthorised dialogue or wrecking her sister's appearance on TV as a Junior Master Chef, Grisel's hilarious adventures will delight children.
ISBN 0 86264 689 8   paperback

WILLY AND THE SEMOLINA PUDDING & Other Stories

'The writing is witty and very funny, the characterisation is sharp and concise . . . Highly recommended for readers of all abilities.' *School Librarian*
ISBN 0 86264 929 3   paperback

WILLY AND THE UFO & Other Stories

Illustrated by David McKee
'Roger Collinson has invented a wonderful character in Willy, an innocent who emerges with distinction from many a bungle.' *Daily Telegraph*
ISBN 0 86264 620 0   hardback